Fax
AND HIS ADVENTURES
TO PREVENT
CLIMATE CHANGE

FAX
AND HIS ADVENTURES
TO PREVENT
CLIMATE CHANGE

L C J Emery

Strategic Book Publishing and Rights Co.

Strategic Book Publishing & Rights Co., LLC
USA
www.sbpra.net

For information about special discounts for bulk purchases, please contact Strategic Book Publishing and Rights Co. Special Sales, at bookorder@sbpra.net.

ISBN: 978-1-68235-768-2

CONTENTS

Chapter One
A SECRET TO KEEP

O ld Father Thyme, as his friends called him, spent most of his life in a little cottage in a village called Seatown. It was a friendly, colourful place to live even in winter, as it was nestled between two hills that were full of dinosaur bones that somehow affected the folk and climate. Before this, he was the lighthouse keeper at Portland near Weymouth, and before that he attended Queen Mary's Elementary School, where he dreamt of becoming a palaeontologist (fossil hunter). The old father had a lovely childhood. He couldn't wish for better parents, as they encouraged the confidence within him so he wasn't afraid to become the person he was meant to be. Considering his age, that was a very long time ago.

As amazing as his family thought he was, it was also his name—Amazing Montgomery Thyme. He was old and frail nowadays, but he managed to keep hold of his hair, and that was all you could see on the pillow in his room of the Old Dinosaurs retirement village. His face held the wrinkles of a beautiful smile that were mostly a product of his wife, children, and the frequent walks up the golden-capped hill, his favourite place.

As he lay dying, though not quite dead, he could still grasp the names attached to the faces that were looking lovingly upon him. His children—sons Trevor, Howard, John, Mark, and Kyle, along with daughters Susan, Alice, Joan, and Sharon—were all wishing for a pain free goodbye. But, unbeknown to anyone, it seemed someone somewhere had different plans for the old father.

It was just before time foretold his death, he remembered himself pottering in this garden, cooking in his kitchen and picnicking with his family. He welcomed his goodbye, as old age didn't come without its inconveniences. He knew he would miss the gift of children, but in passing on to the other side, he hoped maybe he would see the loved one who gave him his children again.

He smiled in his mind, and his hands clenched tightly, as if a corkscrew was about to release his soul.

"One step. Here I go to my final judgement!" he reassured.

His children looked on to what looked like his last intake of breath.

He wondered if he would be greeted with a banner call, with trumpets and horns, or with sniggers and hidden eyes. *Never mind – what will be will be! No longer will I have to endure my sadness toward the harpooning of whales in the magnificent oceans. No longer will I have to be sad for the burning of the rainforests, and no longer will I have to witness suffering that humans inflict on themselves!*

Suddenly, a question popped into his last remaining braincells, asking for help.

Are you asking me what I think you are asking? he thought, cosy but a little strange that, at the end, of all things, there would be one final pub quiz.

A lady's face appeared through his closed eyelids. *Who is this angel?* he thought. She looked beautiful but sad. *Of course, I would help you, but I am dying—nearly dead.*

Suddenly, a sprinkle of cosmic magic entered the old father, and he felt amazing in more ways than one. His muscles felt strong, and his heart began to pound. Then, like a cowboy being thrown through a saloon door, he spiritually entered into unfamiliar surroundings.

"You need to remember, as I have a job for you," said a familiar voice.

Birds were flying. Life was everywhere. Old Father Thyme was confused, but his mind told him it beat dying.

Then he felt it. At first, he felt strong and strangely invincible. His muscles started bulging, and the reassurance of his "Walking frame" melted like ice in a lava pool. He felt fit, fast, and unstoppable. His mind evaporated the cloud cover that had slowly crept in over the years, and he felt that nothing was beyond his understanding.

At first, all Amazing wanted to do was run, as he obviously hadn't done so since he was young. So, he did just that. The angel counted eight thousand back-to-back marathons, and as he did, he glimpsed reflections of his younger self in pools and on shiny surfaces.

"Is everything okay?" the angel asked as she perched herself on a mountain ledge and watched him patiently.

It was at that moment that Old Father Thyme, Young Father Thyme, or just Amazing had a thought. It oozed custard and had a pristine snow-crunch sugar topping. The more he thought about it, the more he wanted it. And the more he wanted it, the more he felt it would become a reality. It came to him via a floury baker's hand.

She counted as he ploughed through three hundred custards slices, 46 chocolate eclairs, 19 roast chickens, a bag of roasted potatoes just like his mother made, three Christmas cakes with thick slices of stilton cheese and drank 37 pints of his favourite ale. She smiled, as she thought he was in a bit of a pickle!

She reminded him that there was something to find, and it was of universal importance. *All I wanted him to do was remember how to use his legs again. He'll come round soon,* she hoped in a mutter.

Amazing ignored her beckoning and started doing star jumps instead. She passed through him, causing a pleasurable outburst.

Suddenly, his mind started playing golf and then sailing on a blue tropical ocean. He drank milkshakes while barbequing. He then he played snooker, volleyball, and rode a motorbike fast. He abseiled, rock climbed, and cave dived as he did when he was a teenager. He nibbled steak and chips while arm wrestling a Sumo wrestler, boxing Mohammad Ali, and then mud wrestled anyone who was willing. He ate crisps while studying mathematics, astrophysics, and geology, sucked marshmallows while looking out from the peak of Everest and chewed wine gums at the bottom of the Mariana Trench.

"Imagination is such wonderment," she muttered to herself as she peeked at the universal clock and noting the time.

Still excited with life's tingling energy, Amazing started to play guitar like Jimi Hendrix. He sang like Meatloaf and played piano like Elton John. He also dabbled with the drums and violin but failed to master the bagpipes.

He found the cure for cancer, dementia, Parkinson's disease, and asthma. He thought himself good looking and attractive. He then ate some whitebait. "Yuk!" He spat it out, and that brought him down to Earth with a bump.

"How are you?" he asked the one being so patient.

"Finally," she muttered. "We have lift off. You missed the vigour of youth, I see!"

"Is this heaven? If it is, I like it," replied Amazing. "Why me?"

"I've been watching you; you're amazing."

"I am," responded Amazing with a cheeky eyebrow.

"Okay, I see some confusion. You're . . . fantastic. You have always put others before yourself, and you have added much understanding to me," she said with enthusiasm.

"But I remember a distant memory," Amazing said worryingly. "I was looking at the white ceiling from my bed, feeling anxious but not frightened."

"Heaven! No, you're still in that bed at the retirement village. You are in my mind now, and I need you to find someone for me, and speed is of the essence."

A clock chimed. "Under the golden-capped hill, you will find what I need," she added.

Amazing could feel himself being pulled back to the bed where he lay. "Who are you?" he asked with his last dimming thought.

2"My name is Methiemauritania, but you can call me Methie."

At the retirement village, Amazing sprang up in bed with a jolt. He felt the world was screaming, the significance of which he couldn't imagine. His children stood back in wonderment. Their father smiled, jumped out of bed naked, and strolled past them signalling to get his clothes.

"It's a miracle!" they shouted.

"You know, one day you are all going to die. You need to live a little while you got a little life left in you. I'm off to see the wizard," their father said in an independent sort of way.

His children were silent as he dressed himself, but then his daughters' faces dropped with a thunderous look, and his boys started to grin, as if to say, "go and have some fun daddykins."

Amazing slipped out the fire escape and ran to his old home, where he muttered the words "cheeky sods" as he snapped up a for sale sign stuck in his garden. He was finding it hard to stay in touch with reality and longed to be back with Methie.

He stood under the wisteria-covered porch not really knowing if he was dead or alive! He wasn't wet, cold, or warm and didn't really feel the need to go inside. He stood thinking about what he needed to find.

Strangely, he felt that he wasn't in the right place. The feeling became stronger and stronger until it pulled him off balance in the direction that felt right. It wasn't far, though, at sea level, or maybe what he needed to find was coming in on the next tide.

The pale moon looked spooky over the ocean, but it was playing its reflective part. Amazing could see the golden-capped hill through the darkness. The golden part was only visible from the ocean, but it felt ironic, as that was the place where he told his family to spread his ashes. He wished the treasure was up there, but a bargain is a bargain, he thought as the lizard man he had seen as a child popped into his mind.

He ran from the wisteria-covered cottage and turned left onto a country lane toward the beach. The sign for the Golden Cap Campsite was approaching, and the Acorn sign to the summit of the hill was on his right. He headed toward the flicking light of the one dinosaur streetlamp that stood at the pebbled beach entrance. Set back was the black-and-white Anchor Pub. He raised a hand in appreciation to the old public house as he passed. He still could describe every picture on every wall, as nothing had changed for hundreds of years. It was the folk who shared the long, cold, quiet nights that he had warmth for, remembering the smiles and songs of friends long gone.

He sped onto the beach, adjusting his feet as he navigated the moving pebbles and looked upon the Jurassic coast that stretched out before him sparkling in the moonlight. The ocean lapped at the shore as though within a lullaby, and he ran as fast as his little legs could carry him.

Methie looked through the moon's eyes and sent her squabbling pet cyclopes to help him. He had some ways to go, and the clouds were closing in. "Speed is what he needs," Methie said to her panting subjects.

Amazing felt an immediate lift, as if someone was running for him. It spooked him a little. He felt a little tickle and then heard a little giggle on the left side of his neck. He glimpsed a multicoloured something. *There it is again,* he thought, *as colourful as a rainbow and smiling!*

The beach ended at a waterfall, where mud and rocks were being carved from the cliff face. Amazing looked in awe. Then there was one mighty thud, with the sound of pebbles being dispersed. It was at that moment that the waterfall trickled to a drop.

Amazing felt the need to act before the sun crawled like a young child appearing at the side of a playground. He subconsciously asked the moon to brighten its reflection, as he needed help to see. He looked within the fallen rocks and moved some pebbles with his feet until he stumbled upon it. He took a double take, as it was unlike anything he had ever imagined. It looked like a cut diamond, but it was its size that had him in a quandary. With conviction that this was what he was sent to retrieve, he bent down to pry it from the land's grasp.

But it was heavy.

Once again, the giggling appeared; this time it gave him the strength that he needed to heave it onto his shoulder and jog back the way he came. The ghostly images of Methie's friendly cyclopes, named Columbia and Peru, had waterfalls streaming down their faces, overemphasizing the fact they had never done a day's work. They took what it was back to the cottage.

Amazing opened the front door of the cottage and then went down to the basement where he placed the massive diamond on his favourite fossilised tree trunk table.

The constant cursing of Columbia and Peru was such that he excepted their ghostly presence and told them to shut up. Methie pulled the squabbling pair back into her realm, as the job was done.

Amazing looked at his old sofa and warmed as he sat, but he knew there wasn't an ounce of time left. He let a memory in. It was Christmas, and all his dear ones sat around the log fire opening presents. He remembered Kyle, his youngest, controlling the burning of the wrapping paper so it wouldn't fall onto the carpet. He smiled, but then suddenly all his happiness evaporated. He felt he wasn't alone but also that he didn't belong. *But I should!* he thought.

There was something behind him. This time it wasn't furry or bright with colours; it was dark and moving. He needed to go. In the basement, he felt cold and his goosepimples shuddered as he stood at the bottom of the stairs and looked up. He felt his strength dwindling, but he had to make it. He took one last look at the diamond and caught a glimpse of a green, lizard-looking chap. He climbed the stairs and moved as fast as he could from the house to the end of the garden. He headed towards the light and found his way back to the retirement village, where his children put him back into his bed.

Amazing looked at his children. "It's okay. I found it. I will go to heaven now." Tears were welling up in their eyes.

Amazing looked at Kyle and prompted him to come closer. He took his ear and said, "In the basement at home is a secret you need to keep. Get word to your professor, and don't touch it until he's there."

Then, Amazing's eyes closed, and he died.

Chapter TWO
KYLE AND THE PROFESSOR

An hour later the family left, having dealt with their initial upset. They gathered in the carpark, where the main topic on everyone's mind turned to Kyle.

"So, what did Father say to you just before he passed?" Susan asked.

"Err . . . what? Sorry, miles away," he responded distantly to the eyes looking at him.

"You have been acting rather strange since his last words," commented Alice.

"Well, yes, we've just lost Dad, and I'm hardly going to jump for joy, am I? They were just ramblings, ramblings of a lovely man!"

"Obviously, it would have been nice to hear what he said," Trevor pointed out.

"Well, until the funeral then," Howard said, changing the subject, much to the agreement of the others.

They said their goodbyes and went their separate ways.

Kyle drove, directly to the cottage. He parked and walked to the front gate. He thought it strange about the for-sale sign but more so about the front door being ajar. He went inside and looked around, leaving the basement to last, cautious of an intruder. The light was already on down below, and so, slowly, he went down, asking if anyone was there.

There was nothing but the large sofa to hide behind. Obviously, the first thing Kyle laid his eyes on was rugby-ball-sized diamond sitting on the fossilised wood table.

"By Jove!" he muttered, wondering if it was what he thought it was. It had to be the biggest in the world. He assumed it must be a crystal.

He smiled at the hundred or so family pictures hung on the walls and noted the solid silver hedgehogs he was fascinated with as a kid were still by the fireplace, but at that moment it was all about whether what he was looking at was a diamond or not.

He moved to touch it, but at the last second, he remembered what his father told him: "Call your professor." His dad was referring to renowned geologist Professor Woodrow Malarkey.

It was 10.13 am, and Kyle knew exactly where he would be. He would be at his place of work, the university, Asteroid Logging, as it was against the professor's moral compass to mine the Earth. As he had always said, "People don't know when to stop, and it will end up like mouse cheese!"

Nevertheless, Kyle rang him. The professor cursed at the inconvenience of the ringing telephone, but he was pleased it was Kyle.

"You do realise the time, Kyle. I think I found another one," the professor answered.

"An asteroid, Professor?" Kyle assumed.

"Not just an asteroid. You know of the gold ones, the silver ones, but this one I've just found is a diamond the size of a house! It's got that light refraction we talked about."

"That's a coincidence, Professor! I'm looking at one the size of a rugby ball, and it's on my dad's table! You need to drop everything and come to me."

"Kyle, I can't drop everything! I've got work to do. I'm sorry about your dad, I really am, but my work needs me here." He paused. "Wait. Size of a rugby ball, you say? At your dad's? Your dad had a diamond the size of the rugby ball? Send me a picture. You must be kidding, right?"

"Kidding? I wish I were. It's already cut, and from some angles it looks like there is a light at its centre."

"A light at its centre? Take a picture!" the intrigued professor repeated.

"I'm trying, but the camera doesn't see it."

"Already cut? Size of a rugby ball? Do you know how much money that would be worth?"

"Professor, I need you down here as soon as possible!"

The professor sensed the urgency in Kyle's voice. Truthfully, he could do with a break, and a little trip to the Dorset coast could be just the tonic.

"Okay, Seatown, Jurassic coast. I've been there before," the professor reassured.

"I'll come pick you up."

"No, my boy, I'm heading for the train station as we speak; I like trains. You can pick me up at Bridport train station."

Hours later

"By Jove, it's real," commented the professor as he eyed the marvel. "It's cut and looks polished. Remarkable! Your dad had it all this time?"

"'Just letting you know,' Dad strangely said, and that I wasn't to touch it until you were here."

"Well, I'm here now, old boy." The professor lunged forward; his arms ready to cradle the stone.

"Whoa!" Kyle gently held the professor back. "Technically, it's still a family heirloom."

"You're rich, old bean. It must be worth one hundred million, easy. God knows what it could fetch if the bloody blighters start a bidding war," commented the professor as Kyle went to pick it up.

"Winston Churchill," Kyle said without thinking, "it's heavy. Can't even budge it."

"Can't be. Impossible." But the professor too was unable to move it. "It must be dense. It's clear though. Usually, diamonds are heavier due to their impurities." He moved his glasses off his head to take a closer look. "Is that the light? It seems to be getting brighter!"

Both Kyle and the professor stood back as it started to glow. Then, to their surprise, the diamond rose in the air and what looked like a body started to form with the diamond at its centre. They wanted to run, but they couldn't.

A creature from the diamond's light stood squinting before them. The shocked faces of Kyle and the professor looked back distorted and petrified. The creature was quick to react, and its next move was to rip their hearts out and hold them beating before them, but a chiming of a child's toy tingled in the mind of the creature, and it had a kind calming effect. It looked around wondering how it could be and questioned its summoning, but its fury was still evident, as its diamond-tipped titanium samurai-like swords were moments away.

But the child's toy played louder in its mind. The beast read Kyle's mind. Afterall, it thought itself not entirely devilish and would show mercy to the one who had released him—at least for a couple of seconds.

Confirming attack mode, it maintained a close-range telepathic link to lock all human brain functions so it could properly assess the situation. Its alien extermination process was activated and started to count down in its head.

Five. A virus to wipe these life-forms from existence was propagated.

Four. The deployment of its virus was readied.

Three. It made plans to circle the planet to kill as many scavenging aliens as he could.

Two. Kyle was his name, and he is the son of Amazing, the human that found you. You love him?

One. What do you mean I love him?

It reached virtually inside himself and switched off the species extermination button and appeared wholeheartedly before Kyle and the professor.

"You are as tactful as a porcupine in a balloon shop!" said the monster in a deep voice. "Have you got something against me? Do you realise I was just sunning myself in the arms of Mini Tikka Moo Moo, my wife?" The monster looked directly into the eyes of the petrified pair.

"Who came up with you?" it added. "You're not alien . . . interesting." It paused to ponder.

Suddenly, the monster thought, *This could be a decoy*. It was looking forward to the barrage of small firearms with thrown grenades. It fancied playing hopscotch with landmines and relaxing while being flamed by a thrower. It scanned its surroundings hoping for hidden enemies. It cursed when it couldn't detect anything. It so wanted a fight, but instead it heard the chiming of the baby toy again. That then changed to a ticking, like a grandfather clock in a grand hall.

"We need to talk," the monster growled as it selected dialogue mode.

Kyle and the professor nervously smiled, as they both thought they had already been eaten. The monstrosity before them that stood on the fossilised wooden table looked like a cross between a shark, a crocodile, and a bulldog. Its voice was deep and hungry.

"Look at your little teeth," said it, peering with blood-red eyes, "and that cute little tuft of hair on your head. I wouldn't fathom to guess how the hell nature came up with you."

The creature felt the need for a smile, but the number of teeth made it impossible to give the right impression. It wasn't only the large spines dripping with blood and the red, possessed-looking snake eyes that scared them to death. It also was the green scales. It had nineteen spines on each leg, two arms with sharp elbows, and hands with pointed fingers for piercing. To top it off, it was bald as a coot.

Kyle blinked and turned to look for guidance from his mentor, but the professor's face said it all, and his eyes were already running.

The monster caught a glimpse of their fear and couldn't understand why their beating hearts were close to failure, and the last thing it wanted was for both of them to die. Concerned, it glanced in the mirror above the fireplace.

"Wow, I do beg your pardon," it said considerately. "I'm not my true self. Whatever must you think of me? This old Crankentorp, I was playing a game, see? Reality, first time see. I've never felt the summonsing before," it said, trying its best to conceal its teeth, but then the creature froze.

Chapter Three
MUD AND ROCKS

The creature stepped inside its quantum and back into its virtual reality where it had spent millions of years. It flung open the dressing room door that housed its costumes, ready for a personality makeover. The blood vanished from its spines.

"Who should I be?" it muttered like an old drama queen, cursing about the boringness and what an absolute tragedy reality was.

There must be something more pleasing to their eye. I'm in the company of fellow earthlings I should look my best, it thought.

It walked down the virtual trailer and began to notice a trend as it went along. The scarier the beasty, the more frequently he had played the part. The dust was the tell-tale sign of a boring life. It stopped at the dustiest! *Maybe a cute and cuddly?* It cleaned a spot to peer inside, but it was dark.

Strange!

The control pad was unreadable. It gave it a little fiddle and pressed a button, and the darkness gave way to dimmed light. It peered through again, but still nothing. It stood back; it could see a reflection of a figure. It was green, muscular, and looked good to the eye (maybe)! *What is this thing?* Suddenly, the booth lit up, the reflection became stronger, and the words "Fax" and "Troodon" appeared. It touched the screen, and a file opened inside its mind.

Oh, my name is Fax, and I am a Troodon. No wonder the poor little humans were about to have a heart attack! It's about time I introduce my true self.

Kyle and the professor looked on as the image of the crocodilian, sharky, and bulldog chap shrank from nine feet to about five. It jumped from the table and stood as if had ended a song. The scales disappeared to become a soft, bumpy sort of texture, and the look of death on its features diminished to something more intelligent looking. Both Kyle's and the professor's hearts started to slow.

"Hi, I must apologise for my appearance; reality is scary. This is the realisation of my true self," Fax said with a wide, cheesy smile, twirling with self-delight. "Greetings, Earthlings. My name is Fax. Maybe a cup of tea?" He giggled.

"W-w-where's the d-d-diamond g-gone?" the professor stuttered

"Diamond . . . yes," Fax said, looking at Kyle. "Your father found me under the golden-capped hill and brought me here. I can't tell how long I've been virtual at the moment, but your father must be remarkable, as my core weighs five hundred kilograms, and basically, I'm a quantum computer made of diamond, so—ha, ha—you're right. Where has the diamond gone?"

"Half a ton? My father was eighty-five!"

"I know. I feel there is more of a story to tell . . . *Tea?*" Fax stared longingly at the pair, as if his request was in a language unrecognisable. Fax again stepped inside his mind, as their response seemed to take an eternity. But Kyle's brain seemed to point toward beer—and lots of it.

"Tea will be fine," Kyle said, ending the uncomfortable standoff. "Of course, I have questions."

"Questions." Fax said with a smile. "I wouldn't have it any other way." Fax virtually stopped his racing mind like horses at the gallop. "I'll make it," he said, overly helpful.

But the professor was quick to react. "By all means, you sit. Relax. I'll go and make it. Just need to nip upstairs, you know. Milk? One lump or two?" he asked, pointing at Fax, but Fax looked puzzled.

"He will have it as I do. Okay?" Kyle pointed out sternly as he felt a breeze and heard a bang from the floor above.

"Be back in a jiffy." The professor's sole purpose as he entered the upstairs was to run, escape, call the police, the fire brigade, the

Royal Society for the Prevention of Cruelty to Animals, anyone who could help, but much to his dismay, the doors and window had been boarded up, and his phone had disappeared. He wandered around the kitchen, head in hands, worried, until he heard laughter coming from the basement.

"So, Fax, you knew my father?" Kyle asked. "Do you know he has just passed?"

"Amazing—lovely man. It was your touch that dragged me kicking and screaming into your reality. Amazing was working for someone else—who that was remains a mystery. He was already dead, or he would have woken me!"

"Already dead?"

"You were meant to wake me. I have checked thirteen million times. Just put it down to an angel."

"An angel?!" Kyle looked delighted.

"An angel, a celestial being, they have always got to interfere. They just can't keep their noses out! My job was to protect the planet from alien intelligence, not from you. Although, I have detected something that could cause a concern."

"What would that be?" Kyle asked.

"All in good time. Not quite sure myself," Fax said calmly.

"When you first appeared, it looked like you were going to eat us."

Fax looked surprised. "First I would have to weigh you!" Fax said, licking his lips. "I would have you cooked. Mmm! Well done would be my preference; none of that rare, medium-to-rare shit. Well bloody done, mate, and only a few bits for starters, the rest I would bin!"

"So, you would eat us?!" Kyle moaned.

"Still thinking about it. Have you changed your underwear recently? No. I'm a bloody vegan, you know, nuts and all that, but I know a million that would eat you!"

"Cool." Kyle looked relieved. "No eating today then!"

"No, not today. Well, look at me. I am egg born; you are honoured."

"Egg born?" Kyle quizzed.

"Hatched from an egg, mate—you know, reptilian. Dino-bloody-soar, your words not mine, mate. Well, I didn't come screaming into this world like you lot, bloody mammals," he said with a giggle. "You're forty-seven years old, and your professor up there is sixty-four years old; I'm still deciphering." Fax paused with wide, humorous eyes.

"Deciphering what?"

"Your bloody brain. The cosiness of warm blood is weird."

"You read my mind? How bloody dare you! I feel naked now," moaned Kyle.

"It's a defence thing. Look, I've been many different creatures before. You spend enough time as yourself, you would get bored too, or go bloody crazy. Look! My existence as the King's Gambit." Fax changed into a pleasant-looking chap, nine feet tall, purple, with a funny lip.

Then he went from King's Gambit to a Bedouin princess. The princess blew Kyle a massive foot-wide kiss, but it was slightly off-putting that she had eight legs.

He then changed into a rockweillier. On top of a pair of inverted legs was a big round ball of a body. It had no arms, and it was cute, but it ate with its ass.

Fax laughed as he reverted to egg born. "See the respect I show you fellow earthlings," he said, stretching out his arms as if to say, "look at my power." But then he quietly and sheepishly mentioned, "I lived as the rockweillier for one thousand years. It's done funny thing to my head—cuckoo!"

"I bet," replied a fascinated Kyle.

"Yes, I admit my entrance was a bit dramatic. The length of time I had been cocooned under the golden-capped hill, I thought there might be aliens!"

"Aliens?"

"I am a member of the Infinite Time Consortium," Fax stated proudly. "I was given the most prestigious of jobs—you know, Kyle—or so they said. The protection of our home world! Stitched up, if you ask me; just in case a planet-eating beasty came wandering our way, I've been listening." Fax's face edged towards anger. "Do you realise how big the galaxy is, let alone the universe?"

Kyle's eyes widened with emptiness. "Not really, Fax. I do mud and rocks!"

"Mud and rocks," Fax said as a cap appeared on his head and shades over his eyes. He chose a long, black, leather coat from his trailer that grew down his arms, ending at fine-fitting gloves that covered his green hands.

The professor started down the stairs with tea and biscuits, but there before him was the Crankentorp again, snarling and voicing about eating him. He dropped the tea and weed himself.

"Sorry, sorry. It was his idea. Sorry." The professor looked at a laughing Kyle. "I told you I would get you back. Remember Cairo? The spider?"

Fax reverted back to egg born.

"That wasn't quite the same," the professor moaned, looking at his wet patch. "I'll go and make some more tea."

Moments later the professor came back down. "I see you have changed," he said, pointing out the obvious.

"Yes, hat, gloves, cool coat, I don't usually indulge, but I got them from Kyle's mind, as I didn't realise at first that I was naked."

"Excellent. Can we go now?" asked the professor almost rudely. "Are we done here? Do you now have everything you need, Kyle, your dads' affairs and all that? Thinking we should head off—traffic, you know."

"No, no rush. Fax is cool; he is different now," noted Kyle.

"Look, Professor, I'm here to help. I was to notify my people of any alien interest the Earth might attract, being that she is blue, lush, and green. You don't realise her beauty against the entirety of space. At first, I thought aliens had invaded, but as it turns out, you evolved here on Earth, and some parts of our DNA are the same."

"So? That is good, yeah?" the professor replied with a German accent. "We can go now."

"I need your help," said Fax. "There is still an unanswered question . . . why?"

"Why what?" the professor asked. "Are you here to pass judgement over us, like that film? Oh, what's it called . . . never mind! How the hell is Fax going to do that? One man—wait, one Troodon—against the world. Who will listen?"

"I just want to understand why I woke," Fax said, smiling.

"A minute ago, I thought you were going to kill us," the professor grunted.

"Well, a moment ago I didn't know you were children of the Earth." Fax winked.

"This is absolutely absurd! I can't and won't betray my fellow man!" the professor shouted.

Kyle tried to calm his friend. The professor was fascinated but wasn't fully convinced about anything. He stood, dithering in his mind.

"Max." The professor demanded his attention.

"Not Max," Fax said with a smile, flexing his jawbone. "I knew a Max once. Never again."

"I am an old man. There must be a really good reason as to why I don't go back to the university. I have papers to mark," the professor said.

"I need you," Fax said with sadness evident in his voice. "Your species needs you; the planet needs you. Times have changed. I cannot walk around. People will see me."

"Yes, they would cut you up and examine you," the professor muttered.

Fax shrugged. "I am indestructible. But I must find out why."

"Why what?" snapped the professor.

"Why I'm here; why there is intelligence. The lessons have been learnt."

"I am not interested in going on a quest of any kind to search for the meaning of life. I'm far too old for all that."

"Intelligence, not life," Fax reminded him.

"What's the difference?"

"A great deal!"

"There is no way!" the professor said, flabbergasted, feeling the conversation was over. "In a wee while," he added with effort, "myself and young Kyle here will be off. We won't tell anyone of our little encounter. Trust me, you will become a distant memory."

Fax moved up to the professor, grabbed hold of his hand, then moved away. "I now know when you are going to die," Fax said.

"Rubbish. How do you know that?"

"Soon," Fax said.

"Soon? What rubbish. I'm as fit as a fiddle. Look!" The professor jumped up and punched the air. He felt a slight pain in his back, but that was nothing unusual.

"You feel pain, old, and tired sometimes. I understand. Your body is old, and your mind is slightly vacant."

"What do you mean vacant, you cheeky sod?" the professor snapped proudly, biting his lip.

"I understand you find it harder to learn as you get older. It takes a little more time for things to sink in," Fax said.

"You're obviously brighter than me, and your understanding of the human condition outweighs my own," replied the professor sarcastically.

"I can take it away."2

The professor looked at him in fear. "I don't want to die just yet, thank you."

"Not dying. Here, take my hand."

The professor stretched out his hand without thinking, and Fax took it. He held it for about ten seconds as he looked into the professor's eyes.

"God! Blimey!" Kyle said after seeing what Fax had done. "Take a look at yourself."

The professor was smiling, as he knew something was up. He had never felt so young and alive.

"What have you done?"

"It's simple when you know how," Fax said.

The professor looked in the mirror over the fireplace. "Not only do I feel it, I look it as well!"

"Your biological age is Thirty. Thirty-four years have been removed. I hope you don't mind."

"Don't mind? I will help you, without question!" beamed the professor.

"What about me?" Kyle asked. "I'm not helping you. Look at you, Professor. You look magnificent."

"You not going to help?" Fax asked.

"Yes, well . . ."

"Okay," Fax smiled. He took Kyle's hand and held it for the same length of time.

Kyle rushed to get the mirror, tussling a bit with the professor. Kyle looked in the mirror and saw a fitter self. He felt good but was a little puzzled. He looked at Fax.

"Oh, you have the body of a marathon runner, and all cellular damage has been reversed. You would probably live to about two hundred, if left to its own devices and you ate your veggies," Fax explained.

"Oh, thanks!" Kyle said. "I will help you!"

Chapter Four
WHAT'S UP WITH FAX?

Kyle's campervan was full of laughter, had bouts of silence and crazy green lizard conversations as it chugged its way back to the university. Their lives had changed. It was like they were caught in a constant champagne moment since feeling younger and found they couldn't wait to see Fax again.

Meanwhile back at the cottage, Fax had the opportunity to figure out why he had been so rudely confronted with reality.

Fax was vexed but calm with it. He contemplated his complexities and found a fondness for Kyle and could see them both becoming great friends—if this friends thing was what he understood it to be. Obviously, holding somebody's beating heart in front of them doesn't amalgamate a good friendship, and this he had to understand. In his virtual world, anything goes. Reality, for the moment anyway, needed a constant pinch. There was always the risk he could forget and not realise which was which and go on the rampage!

Heaven forbid, he thought sarcastically. *I could get arrested and thrown in jail if I get it wrong.*

Fax also held a high five for the professor—so much so that he felt a bit guilty towards the wee thing and this scaring people to near death. It was funny though! But Fax came to realise he was the only one with pause, rewind, and fast-forward buttons. It was kind of obvious, but he really had to think about it and remember who he was in reality, as the thought of shooting somebody and not being able to rewind would weigh heavy on his mind. He just had to remember the good guy he was, a member of the Infinite Time Consortium, and after all, this friends thing wasn't a new concept. When Fax was alive, as well as hidden somewhere in a quiet forgotten part of his quantum brain, Mini was forever playful. His life wife, his virtual wife, his love. He wasn't quite sure if she existed anymore, but if she became an infinite, he would find her, and he knew just whom to ask.

Whom to ask was the same Troodon that found him millions of years ago. Although he had a suspicion of whom he shared his DNA with, everything was a closely keep secret. His headmaster knew all, and he also knew how everything came to be. Fax would have been left in the swamps of the then Earth if it wasn't for him.

"That was the making of you, boy," his master would say. "A hatchling's potential is governed by its cunningness in avoiding being eaten by the large nasties that want to eat you!"

Obviously, Fax wasn't gobbled up. Instead, he started riding the swamp creatures that showed him their bright, shiny teeth. It was at that moment he was coached from the bogs and into the classroom by said headmaster. There, he exceled in his schoolwork, gave up the croc riding, and started riding tyrannosaurus rexes instead, and his favourite was called Meower.

Fax now thought it completely logical to keep things as normal as possible, and he agreed with Kyle and the professor before they left that he could watch TV, have access to the World Wide Web and listen to some music. He walked about the kitchen and bedrooms as if it was his own home. He caught a glisten from the early evening sun through the kitchen window and pondered sitting in the garden, but then he saw the hat of Mrs Barber. Kyle had mentioned something about the nosey neighbour. He ducked before she raised a nose over the fence. There was no way he was ready to be seen; and what if she raised a curious wave? Her extermination wouldn't go down well, so he sneaked back into the basement, as reality wasn't ready for him quite yet.

He turned on the music player, selected random play and popped about the basement, looking at all the pictures as he went. It wasn't long before he was fed up, as the words didn't really allow for dance as Kyle said the radio would; it was more about news.

By this time Fax was becoming disenchanted, so he lay on the floor with his head on the fireplace, looking up through the chimney, bored. The hole was round, sooty and blued at the sky. He lay there for an hour numbing to reality, but he couldn't help but think about the nosey neighbour.

She could climb on the roof and look down on him at any moment. Although remote, he thought it was possible. So, he had to move. But as he did, he come face to face with the hedgehogs that were on the hearth. They held a wonderment in Kyle's memory, but to him it was like coming face to face with a venomous snake. His quantum triggered an alarm, and all the signs were saying that silver was a demon to him. But what was more intriguing was that it reminded him of something he had in his pocket—something he had stolen without even knowing, and it far outweighed Kyle's fascination with silver hedgehogs—and the professor hadn't noticed it missing . . . yet!

"What's AU seventy-nine?" Fax muttered. "Ha ha! It's only eighteen carats though," he replied without thought.

Suddenly, Fax felt a hurricane brew in his mind, and he knew it was the damn silver that had triggered it. It was worse than a migraine and alluded to an addiction.

He collapsed on the floor as the longing became so strong. He couldn't understand; it was corrupting. He needed what it was but didn't know why. It was uncontrollable, but as soon as he thought it, he knew via Kyle's mind where he could find it. He had the impression it only came from supernovas and somehow understood the power contained inside it was massive. But Fax was told, back when he was alive, in the time of schooling that what it was wasn't to be found on this planet, and for the first time he realised the teachers who schooled him were all liars.

Fax was concerned about his low-power mode and made his way to the fossil table. He turned on the TV Kyle had set up for him and flicked through channels.

Gold rush, gold fever, panning for gold, digging for gold, mining for gold and gold leaching . . . humans are obsessed with gold, he thought as channel after channel broadcast how people went about getting the stuff. Ocean dredging and deforestation was a cause of concern to him, so much so that he linked up to the World Wide Web to gather more information.

By this time, the music had changed. Fax noticed and started tapping his foot.

He saw pictures of jungles being burnt, trees being logged, land being ripped up, people being shot, flaming furnaces, oceans being dredged, animals being slaughtered, extinction events, wars, roads gridlocked with cars, factories pumping endless fumes, plastic waste covering both land and sea, turtles dying, and food chains dying because of plastic pollution and overfishing.

Fax was getting angry as the images flashed faster in his quantum. The beat of the music seemed to go with it, and the words "This means war with your creator" were as poignant as ever.

Then it was tanks, container ships, warships, submarines, planes, helicopters, chemical factories, farms being sprayed, dead insects, dead farm animals, guns, roadkill, people drugged, nuclear power stations, coal power stations, oil production plants, fracking, fishing boats, bombs exploding, gas burning, ice caps melting, methane venting, surgeons operating, space shuttle flying, first boot on the moon.

The musical beat was encouraging, and the words "simulations, algorithms, push us aside, render us obsolete, and war with your creator," were making sense to Fax.

Now it was babies being born, America, Russia, United Kingdom, France, China, India, Pakistan, North Korea, Belgium, Germany, Italy, Netherlands, Turkish flags, nuclear weapons. Fax stood up, disconnecting himself from the internet, took the gold ring that he stole from the professor from his pocket and ate it.

He screamed to the finial lyrics, "This means war with your creator!" as the song beat out.

By now it was the twilight, and Fax suddenly felt power that could not be contained. He zoomed from the cottage out over the ocean and into space. He was getting angrier as his quantum repeated those images. He could foresee that people were so endemically destructive that logic dictated they were going to create a planet where life wouldn't survive.

Again, he calculated the order in which he thought seven billion people could die. But it was at that moment a thought popped in his head, along with the sound of that baby toy again. He was over docklands, where he noticed that the largest container ship in the world was berthed. He flew down and lifted the container ship out of the water, balancing it in one hand. His quantum calculated the flight path and force he needed to send it out of the atmosphere to find his bullseye. He threw it like a quarterback, with such force that the quay wall cracked under his feet. It was out of sight within a heartbeat. It skimmed orbit as its bow started to glow. It cut through the atmosphere, and a few containers evaporated in an explosion as they fell off the back. The ship was close to also burning up, but as it grew hotter, it nosedived and embedded itself point first into the heart of the Yellowstone Park's supermassive volcano.

Fax cheered as he realised his bullseye, but as soon as he did, he became worried, as he was unclear why it was his bullseye.

Suddenly, the gauge measuring his power status floored as he flew over Ukraine. He was flying on mere atoms and spluttered his way back to the Swiss cottage, so much so that he fell from the sky and landed in the garden, setting off a couple of car alarms in the area. He picked himself up, apologising under his simulated breath, and stumbled as if drunk back down into basement, where he sat giggling. He could picture people's faces, wondering how the hell did a container ship get to where it was. He chuckled at the power of the supernova and gold being his superpower. He also laughed at his new sense of purpose. It was as the song said: "War with the creator!" And Fax's war was going to be with the creation of Metal."

Chapter Five
WORLD NEWS EVENT

The next morning was slow to arrive, as Kyle had restless legs and didn't properly drift into RNS sleep until around 5am. It was Tuesday when his alarm woke him at 7am. So, it was business as usual, he thought as he lay there trying to find a loving thought to counteract the hatred towards the alarm. But it only took a second before greenie popped into the forefront of his mind. He probably dreamt about him, but he couldn't remember. He jumped out of bed and said "yippy" a number of times, thanking the sunlight for the waking day. He showered, dressed, breakfasted, and walked out the door towards the university. His one-bedroom flat was only a hop, skip and a jump away, so there was no need for the combustion engine, and that was just the way he liked it.

At the university, Kyle made his way through smiles, hellos and condolences that accompanied the corridors. He was on his way to his lab, which was up the creaky staircase. It creaked because it was old, as the builder three hundred years ago never got round to bricking it. At the top was a belfry, and at its middle was the door to the crusty sanctum. In there were samples of every rock known to science, which were displayed or filed away in hundreds of drawers.

Kyle walked in and said hello to the resident cat, Alan, whom nobody claimed to own. He was on the windowsill. He also said hello and sprinkled some food into the tank for his goldfish, Steve. The floor moved with spiders as he sat at his desk and puffed; his lack of enthusiasm was evident as he peered through some papers he needed to mark. He was offered compassionate leave because of his dad and all, but he thought it best he kept busy.

Kyle was very starey that morning. He looked about the books that stretched from floor to ceiling, and at the crystals and volcanic and metamorphic rocks. The array of diamonds just made him chuckle, as their value seemed to be insignificant. He flicked the kettle on for the fifth time, determined to take a break. His foot pressed the plunger that opened the secret cupboard and switched the TV on. It was almost lunchtime, and through nibbles of a chocolate biscuit the BBC announced it had breaking news.

The presenter on the television said, "We would like to interrupt this program to go over to Ajax Tavern, who has a strange story concerning a container ship that has been found in the middle of Yellowstone National Park in the United States of America."

Kyle spat out his biscuit and listened intently.

"Hello, this is Ajax Tavern, ABC News, reporting from Yellowstone National Park, Wyoming, in the United States. I am here at the Ranger's ranch with Arizona Cardinal and girlfriend Strawberry Lane; they contacted me earlier about a bazaar finding that they stumbled across."

The camera turned to the pair wearing red-checked shirts, jean shorts, and hiking boots.

"Can you tell me in your own words what actually happened?"

Strawberry pinched Arizona to say she would explain. "Well, it's like this. It was about three am that I awoke to a swirling sound and whistling in the sky. It sounded a bit like a kettle boiling, but it got so loud that I thought it was going to explode, until there was a silence that ended with a big thud. The ground shook a bit.

"As you can tell by my eye bags, I couldn't get to sleep after that! So, at first light I crawled out of the tent and looked out over Yellowstone. The unspoilt views we were hoping for were beautiful, but then I noticed in the distance a strange shape. I woke Arizona up," she said with a little giggle, "and he confirmed through his camera it was, like I told you via email and phone, a container ship in the middle of Yellowstone! But what I couldn't understand was that there is no sea!"

The camera turned to back to the news reporter, Ajax. "There you have it, folks. How indeed did a Chinese container ship end up in the middle of Yellowstone. If it wasn't for these young explorers that have been hiking on and off for three days, we would never have come to know. The picture confirms what they saw. It's a container ship of Chinese origin. They couldn't believe it at first and started questioning. Rightly so! It's something the world will also ask.

"The campers called the rangers through old volcano watch telephone system. Now we have with us park rangers Ted Huggy and The Bear. Can you tell us the happenings of earlier and what you believe to be the reason behind the container ship?"

"Well, good morning, Ajax. Good morning, America, and good morning the world," Ted said as he ran his hand through his hair, relishing being in the spotlight at last.

"Can you tell us your side of this remarkable story Ted?" Ajax asked, holding the microphone.

"Yes, well, it wasn't there yesterday I'm telling you! The telephone rang early, and it was Strawberry. I thought it unusual because it was on the old watch system. Firstly, I looked at the seismometer and thanked the maker! I picked up the receiver and, in her sweet voice, she told me to stop slacking, solider, and get outside, as there was something I needed to see. I thought this here little lady was crazy at first when she said what it was in the middle of the damn park. I simply said, 'I don't believe it.' I put the receiver back and sat back in my chair, thinking about kids nowadays.

"But then the Bear over there," the camera focused on ranger two; he was a smiling big man, "overheard and confirmed they phoned from high point number one, and you get a good view of the whole park from up there. So, that kind of changed my mind. So, we took the truck up Grizzly Pine Pass; you get a good view from up there too," he said, nodding. "And that is when we called the sheriff, cause through those binoculars I could make out the letters COSCO on the side. It's like God has been playing darts with container ships! We phoned the sheriff's department at eight am, just before you arrived." Ted smiled as he pulled a bemused face at the camera.

The camera turned to Ajax again. "And so it remains a mystery how a Chinese container ship has ended up at Yellowstone National Park. We have been informed that the president is also concerned and promises that he will use all his power to find the person or country responsible for this. This is ABC News; Ajax Tavern reporting."

Kyle phoned the Swiss cottage. Fax intercepted the phone signal, but there was eerie silence.

Chapter Six

MAPS

"Fax, was that anything to do with you?" Kyle asked as if he already knew the answer.

"Kyle, it drove me mad!" Fax answered.

"What do you mean mad? Have you seen the news?!"

"What news?" Fax seemed a touch sheepish.

"You're connected to everything?"

"I've been sleeping. I'm not myself," moped Fax.

"You don't sleep."

"I do. I mean, I have. I don't know. I feel low." Fax noticed an indicator flashing in his peripheral vision indicating low power.

"So, you had nothing to do with the container ship?"

"Container ship, what containerrrrr s-s-ship?" The phone fell dead.

The conversation ended with a dull drumming sound. Kyle quickly tidied up, fed Steve again, and hid anything to do with the TV.

"How strange," he muttered. Kyle shook his head with the bazaar thought. He grabbed his rucksack and sped down the stairs, leaving the door ajar, apologising to the timber as it creaked.

Professor Woodrow Malarky was always hard to find. He hurried through corridors of smiles and waves until he came to the room of the mind— the Staff Room. He quicky peeped in, but the professor wasn't sitting where he usually was. So, he asked Professor Ruby in a puffed-out way, "A volcanologist Woodrow romanced from time to time, where could he be?"

She looked at the clock. "He's under doctor's orders. You'll probably find him at Dicky Stomachs."

Kyle apologised to the nurse as he entered the examination room. He looked at the professor, who smiled, and within a nanosecond of embarrassing eye movement, Kyle agreed to wait outside.

Ten minutes later the professor appeared.

"Thank God you're fully dressed! I think I'm scarred for life now."

"Well, got to have a good flushing every week; good for the soul."

"Fax said think young," Kyle pointed out. He probably didn't need a good flushing anymore.

The professor looked around, thought young, and became young. "Old habits!" he said and returned old, giggling.

"I think Fax is dead," Kyle explained.

"Dead?! I thought he was indestructible. The container ship at Yellowstone, I assumed that was him!"

"He denied it, but he said something about being driven mad."

"Well, we better go and find out!"

With all said and done, Kyle and the professor made their way via Kyle's old VW camper down to Seatown.

They pulled up outside the wisteria-covered cottage and inside found Fax lying on the floor. There was no moving him, but Fax knew they were there. He opened his eyes and immediately sprang to his feet, a little bit unbalanced.

"Hello, guys, feeling a bit ill lately; head is in a bit of a pickle."

"You're okay then? Nothing to report?"

Fax's face looked like was caught in car headlights. He started to bite his teeth together, but his lips started to mouth words. He turned his back as his facial muscles sharpened. He was determined his voice box not create the soundwaves to answer. He turned from an ill-looking pale green, to dark green, and then, looking like a ripening tomato, he couldn't hold it anymore.

"Yeah, I lost it a bit with that container ship. You should be glad I didn't carry out what I had planned first." Fax laughed. "I wish I could see their faces. Funny, the president of United States and China have put the military on high alert." Fax laughed louder.

"This is serious, Fax," pointed out the professor.

"Serious my ass; you shouldn't have left me alone with your trash," Fax said, pointing at the electronic equipment. "You're to blame, polluting me with that. No wonder it's corrupting my quantum."

"We better stay with you then, until you are well," Kyle said with a disagreeable sound coming from the professor, who was looking around for some reason.

"I lost my wedding ring the last time I was here. I'm sure of it. Have you seen it, Fax?"

"No. What does it look like?"

"Gold."

"Gold, AU seventy-nine." Fax started to drool. His face turned possessed. Even the thought of it made him strong. "It's true. I can't stay here any longer." Fax then ate Kyle's and the professor's mobile phones, much to their bewilderment.

Fax then changed his appearance to a hooded human. With black hair and strong cheek bones, he was pleasant looking. "Time to think yourselves young." He clapped his hands, tapped his feet, and shimmied along the shiny hall floor to the latched door, as if confident that everything was going to plan.

In the garden, Fax looked toward the old hippy love camper, and then looked toward Kyle and the professor for conformation that it was the transportation, but as Fax got inside, the tyres burst, and the chassis hit the ground.

"We need a bigger car," the professor said with a giggle as Kyle looked on, defensively referring to it as a classic.

Fax ordered a limousine, transferred the driver one million pounds whilst pickpocketing his wedding ring, and told the professor to drive.

Fax was bolstered into action—well, at least he was moving and not stuck in that basement. He realised he was more conformable with company, but still the puzzle was puzzling. Someone was playing with him. It was like he was under the command of a higher-ranking officer.

"This takes the freedom out of travel," Fax said as he analysed the air. "Fuelled by ancient life," he moaned and couldn't believe he was even entertaining travelling in a vehicle created by some tree-hopping, water-guzzling, methane-filled, beautiful-but-not-so-bright airheads. "This atmosphere compares to five volcanoes erupting for the last thousand or so years."

Fax vibrated as he spotted some roadkill. Suddenly, flashes of dead animals killed by cars streamed through his quantum. He lay on the back seat staring out the window, silent, as if the roadkill was too much to handle. It all pointed to the fact that reality was hard work, and he already craved a vacation. He wanted to go back to where he had been for millions of years, back to his virtual cartoon reality.

Selfishly he dived in, and Fax became Queen Abduction of the Lunaticus planetary system. She was a freedom fighter from the autumn forests on an asteroid called Seven. She was surrounded and under heavy fire and was aware of her failings. Fax flicked through her weaponry for one last fight. There was no way she was going to be taken alive. Then he came to it, the genocide gun. It was a laser weapon that, if used, could help her survive the ambush. He pressed the trigger and fell into the parlours of the seventeen sisters of the great Galilei; they were very, very seductive. He smiled at the possibility.

Suddenly, Fax felt reality and returned to claustrophobia. He put his hand in front of where Kyle was tapping his head.

"Were you sleeping?" Kyle asked.

"Kind of. I go everywhere but nowhere, baby!" Fax said as he pressed his bored face firmly against the back window.

The gorge tailed off into the darkness of the night sky. Suddenly, Fax's attention became very heightened, and he pushed his head through the back window, shattering the glass. He stood up as Kyle and the professor questioned what the hell he was up to.

"Brunel's suspension bridge," Kyle pointed out, brushing shattered glass off his shoulder.

"Gold, lots of gold!" Fax pined.

"You have got a bad case of gold fever about you!" the professor said, laughing.

"Is this the city of gold?" Fax asked. "I've seen it on the mammal net!"

"City of gold? There be tons of gold, Fax, stored in banks I expect," commented Kyle.

The professor looked up. "If gold is what you want, Fax, you could steal the crown jewels," he said with a touch of sarcasm.

Fax immediately clicked through the locations of what the professor was referring to. His jaw dropped, and his tongue flopped like a dog panting.

Kyle clocked this; he had an inclination that his father's find was indeed powerful. How much and what Fax's true intensions were was still a mystery, but Kyle was still all-trusting. After all, he hadn't killed anyone yet, but the news of the container ship was still thundering around the globe, and the consequences were still a mystery.

Then, something hit Fax like a brick in the bath. He usually wouldn't worry about it, but the nattering in his quantum was going to cause irritation if he ignored it. He floated out above the car, telling Woodrow and Kyle that he would find them later.

Fax wanted to do two things. Firstly, to go to the golden-capped hill and visually inspect the land as he flew. He slipped the ring from the limo driver in his mouth but nearly fell from the sky, as it was only nine-carat gold. He started coughing and spluttering as he separated it, spitting the copper and nickel out so fast that it blew up a truck's engine.

"Whoops!" Fax muttered into the night sky.

Three minutes later, Fax returned to the car as they started driving up the university's road. "These are the visions I have been having," Fax muttered sad-like. "Lines everywhere."

"Lines?" Woodrow commented without thought.

"Roads," explained Kyle. "I think Fax is a bit of an environmentalist."

"Yes, roads for cars, ancient energy, driven by humans, cutting up the land and destroying life." Fax sat back. "Just an observation," he added, looking up the word Kyle had said.

"We're doomed."

"Poppycock," replied Woodrow. "He's in need of some cheering up, that's all."

"What? What?" Fax heard this *cheering up* and zoomed back to reality. "That reminds me," he said. "Where is this bank?"

Kyle looked worried.

Up the hill was the University of Earth Sciences. Fax saw it as a magnificent structure that really was only to keep rain off human heads.

These must be shops. Fax recalled Kyle's mind as he saw him having a meal with Fiona, a girlfriend of the past, in the Sapphire Fire curry house. Fax was so interested that he homed in on all the menus hung on the windows enticing people in. There was such a selection. Chicken, pork, duck, beef, lamb, prawn, cod, mackerel, snapper, bream, swordfish, tuna, haddock, halibut, salmon, sardines, pomfret, monkfish, trout, crab, lobster, crayfish, shark, and mussels were available across ten restaurants going up the hill.

Fax let his quantum bring what he was thinking to the forefront of his mind. He didn't know if it was his own personal thinking or not; all he knew was that thoughts instigate actions, and actions can cause chaos.

The world's oceans are taking the brunt of this population explosion, said a consciousness unfamiliar.

"I agree!" Fax replied in his quantum.

The land isn't as diverse as when I was alive.

"Yes, I agree!"

No drought could have done this; it's too constructed.

"Highly possible!"

Why have they destroyed the woodlands?

"Me not know. It's crazy!"

They don't realise trees support all life?

"They can't be that bright!"

What are you going to do, Faxy?

"What do you mean? Apart from kill everyone, I haven't given it a thought."

Death is silence. You're not going to imprison me again, said the unfamiliar consciousness.

"Who are you? You are making me angry; show yourself!" Fax urged.

Angry? Ha! Remember the baby toy? The baby toy tinkled into silence.

Fax felt the engine come to a complete stop, and it kind of brought him round. The professor parked the limousine around the corner and told Fax he was looking forward to showing him around, but Fax had a more pressing concern on his mind. He could smell it. He could almost taste it. It was coming from the museum next door. It was in the basement under high security, and it was as pure as pure could be. He tiptoed all sneaky-like until he looked at it with such delight. He put his hand to the glass and shattered it, setting off the alarm. He could sense he was being watched by cameras, so he stood in the corner and bit little pieces off of it until his eyes grew brighter. It was lovely, but for Fax, this was a mere snack. He remembered what the professor had said. It was possibly rude, he thought, to simply up and leave, but resistance was futile where Fax and gold were concerned.

Fax flew to London faster than a bullet, and he was just about to feast on the world's most prestigious treasure when the consciousness made its entry again.

After a little confusion, he found what he was looking for and hovered a hundred feet up in the air, finding shadow. There were two policemen guarding a big black gate, and the cobbled street behind was called Downing Street. Fax needed to talk to the person who resided in Number 10. Before he thought, he shot a laser from his left eye, which exploded the car just far enough so that he could fly over the gate undetected. He stood in front of the black door contemplating whom he should be. He banged the door, and the prime minister answered, dishevelled and still in his longs.

"Sir David Attenborough, what the devil are you doing here? Got no problem and all that, old bean, but how the devil did you get past the officers? It's six am! No chance I've messed this up. How strange! Do come in."

"Why thank you, Prime Minister. We need to talk."

The prime minister had a worried shocked look on his face; he looked as if he could trust the world-renowned TV presenter but was extremely puzzled by his presence.

"Who is it, dear?" asked a voice from the stairwell.

"My wife," he pointed out. He walked to her and explained everything was okay, but whispered, "Call security and let them know we have a guest."

"Right, David, shall we go to the study a bit early for tea? What indeed seems to be the problem?"

"Well, I have been telling you for years about the impact you humans have been having on the planet, and you have done nothing about it. Climate change, habitat loss, processes that have taken millions of years that you humans wipe out in seconds."

"Woah, woah. Just hold it there, old man. I could have you arrested. These are complicated issues, and they will be addressed one day, I'm sure."

"Maybe, Prime Minister, but not by you. I'm here to tell you that I'm going to do it." David-o-Fax looked at him directly, as if to say there will be no fooling around this time. And with their eyes locked in a serious stare, Fax flashed them reptilian!

"Ah!" The British prime minister stepped back with a disgruntled, surprised look. Then it occurred to him. "I see," he said, waggling his finger. "Container ship?"

David-o-Fax smiled. "I've got a lot funnier things lined up." He giggled.

"Just how did you transport a container ship to Yellowstone National Park overnight?" the British prime minister asked with delicate curiosity.

"I threw it!"

"Right. Okay . . . you have my undivided attention!"

"I've come up with a plan. She wants deer to be able to run from John o' Groats to Land's End without being hindered by any roads or man-made complications.

"She? Who's she?" pondered the prime minister.

"My boss! This is the map; the line is ten miles wide at its maximum, and within that I will remove everything man-made and plant forests," David-o-Fax explained.

"And how do you propose we do that? This is absolutely preposterous. I simply won't allow it!"

"Allow it? Hey! There is no 'not allowing it' anymore! I am allowing it. You don't seem to understand that I'm under curfew, being bossed about, under the thumb. Somebody has got my balls in a vice, and they are ready to squeeze!"

"Who is it? The Americans, the Chinese, or the royal family?" asked Bertie, the British prime minister.

Fax appeared reptilian, and the prime minister smiled respectively. "It's your children and the unborn that I work for. Do you honestly think I'm scared of you airheads? I am Fax the Invincible! And if I had my way, I would kill every last one of you milk suckers!"

"I see. Well, I'm glad you have your balls in a vice, if that is the case!" said the very-well-spoken prime minister.

Fax then explained that on the seventh night from now his plan would hatch. The prime minister was to evacuate everyone within the red borderline on the map, or else there would be no telling their experience. Fax tried to explain his avoidance of towns and cities, but Oxford, Coventry, Bradford, Falkirk, and Stirling had it rough. Every road and railway track was going to be dug up and river bridged for every deer, hedgehog, and worm. There was no escaping this, and it all would be done in one night. "Starting with this country," Fax pointed out.

"Who do you think you are? The king of the world?" demanded the prime minister.

"King, queen, I'm everything," Fax replied as pictures of kings and queens entered his head. He then became feverish and fled from

Downing Street to beyond the clouds, trying to get a grip. He finally put those pictures out of his mind, helped by nibbles of gold. Now he felt more determined than ever, so that day he spent giving maps to every leader of a country he or his unfamiliar consciousness felt needed one.

Chapter Seven

THE PLANNED MURDER OF DAVID ATTENBOROUGH

David-o-Fax visited forty-seven countries that day. He zoomed here, there and everywhere, introducing himself to the countries' leaders. There seemed to be a method to his madness, as the mention of Yellowstone had their jaws dropping and them intently listening. He told them all about his plans for wildlife corridors, and they had no choice but to rejoice in this.

The last county he visited, as close to six am as possible, was Finland. He was quite disappointed, from a dictator's point of view, that he didn't have to lay the nut on any of them, but there was one that came close.

David-o-Fax landed at the home of the Finnish president, noted the time, and felt a relaxation enter his nova drive. He was aware of his depleted power and didn't really want to fall from the sky again, so he took a bit of time and nibbled on some of the Salmiakki that the Finnish president had offered. It was a liquorice flavoured with salmiak salt. He was polite even as skull and crossbones flashed throughout his quantum, as he couldn't stomach another wheel. He took her hand and wished her farewell. He could still manage a few loop-the-loops as he few through the sky but ate her wedding ring as well just in case.

He flew south above the clouds, noticing Greenwich as he passed. He didn't really know where he was going, but Seatown was where he was drawn.

He clocked the moon for confirmation of the time spent in his virtual world. By his calculations, it was sixty-six million years, just before the asteroid crashed, but fuzzy were his recordings. The professor was right, and he was kind of savouring the moment, in an English gentry sort of way.

"What would people think of me?" he muttered as he understood their value.

He landed in the garden, noting the next-door neighbour was still in bed, and popped to the basement. He couldn't fully relax, as the motivation behind the life corridors was still vexing his quantum.

Was it himself? Or was there someone else controlling his conscience, brainwashing him into action? He understood the hardware at his disposal could make anything possible, but he knew that the task he had presented to Bertie and the world was astronomical.

"It's like I am employed but not getting paid," Fax muttered while sat on the fossilised wood.

He started to playing Space Invaders while he listened in on the secret communication of the leaders of the world. The topic of wildlife corridors was rife, and . . . was David Attenborough still alive?

Also, does he think he is king of the world?

Also, how is he going to do it?

Also, how are the people going to cope?

Also, what a good idea!

But mostly from the least hedgehog-healing nations were the concluding words: "The worldwide naturalist David Attenborough must die."

Fax giggled at the British prime minister's attempts to tell them that he wasn't human, that he was a quantum invincible being from the past.

Fax lay in his light and fluffy haven, the games console smoking due to his high score. He started to view pictures of kings and queens in his mind.

"These surroundings aren't quite me," he muttered into daylight.

Fax booked himself on the guided tour of the Tower of London, but before joining the queue, he popped to where he was found, under the golden-capped hill. His presence automatically gave him access to a vast network of ancient tunnels. Fax fitted his hand into a carving on the wall, and with a low hum, light lit up the tunnels. Everything looked machine-like. He pulled his hand out from the terminal, and the tunnels fell back into darkness. Fax was happy, as he had confirmed his calculations.

He flew from the beach, loop the looping, to join the queue at the Tower of London. He stood handsome, high-cheek-boned, black hair, cool shades, black shirt, pink flamingo shorts, and flip-flops. He constructed the knobbiest of knees, as he loved knobby knees. He smiled politely to the Beefeater as he walked through the tower gate and fitted in just rightly as he started the tour.

He was told of the thousand-year history, that William the Conqueror had the tower built when he defeated the Romans. He nodded at the portcullis and shuffled his feet down Mint Lane, where he was handed a polo. He danced the shimmy into Water Lane and tutted at Traitors Gate and said, "Naughty." He caught a smile from a pretty lady to his left. Fax could have thrown up; mammal loving was not on his agenda!

Fax thought about blowing his cover and heading straight for the crown jewels, but he decided at the last moment to keep up the charade. He could see them through the walls; he was getting excited. He stuck his tongue out at Blood Tower and bowed his head as if ashamed of chopping off heads of the past. The cobblestones that led up to the White Tower and the Waterloo Block were next. Fax was concealing his excitement very well, but his naughty side was screaming.

He smiled at the armed guards as he entered the jewel house. He stood silent and was unable to move. Within a second, he noted there was 142 items, including thirteen crowns, six swords, and six sceptres and orbs. Fax also immediately knew that this could fuel him for most of his plan. Then he could slip back into his virtual reality.

He stood in front of the biggest crown. He couldn't imagine anything so beautiful being done with supernova power. He put his hand through, shattering the bomb-proof glass. Alarms sounded as he placed the St Edward's Crown on his head. A gun was then thrust in his face. Tour members started running about. But Human-o-Fax wasn't fazed; it was like he was drunk on champagne. He calmly flattened the muzzle of the SA80 machine gun of the Royal Fusilier who had been loudly shouting about shooting him. The ginger-haired weapon-wielding guard looked at the muzzle and backed away. Fax's eyes started to swirl, as the gold was so glittering; he felt like he was home at last.

Outside the jewel house was commotion, and armed personnel gathered. Fax delicately picked up an orb, holding it in his left and the sceptre in his right. It looked like it suited him as shouts rang through his ears. "Somebody is trying to steal the crown jewels!" One hundred people gathered outside, twenty of them uniformed and holding machine guns.

Fax, overwhelmed with the beauty, stumbled and staggered out of the jewel house, still wearing the crown. The twenty machine guns raised and pointed at him; he smiled as if he didn't know what the fuss was about.

Human-cheek-boned Fax slurred, "I really lovvve gollld. Look howww pretty you've made it. You're so clevvverrr!" He stumbled, flapping. "Noww thiss is myyyy hooouse," he added. "Gettttt outtt the lotttt of youuu."

The soldiers took aim with their rifles, as if Fax was going to be executed. The leader asked the thief to lay facedown on the floor. When he didn't, he fired a bullet at his leg. Fax didn't even register the noise.

"My goolllld! Getttt out of myyyy housse!"

"This is a royal palace, sir, and I must insist you lay on the floor facedown." The leader of the Royal Fusiliers shot him in the other leg. The shooter looked at his gun as, again, Fax didn't register being shot. People started to disperse, as they could tell something wasn't right. Some said it could be a show or training, but most were on their way out. The fusiliers were ordered to stand fast, but you could see worried looks under their berets.

"Right, sir, you have your warning, for king, queen and country." The leader pulled the trigger of his pistol, noting the recoil, which aimed at the thief's heart. Fax's smile continued as he gave the order to fire. Each machine gun fired one shot.

Again, Fax's smile continued but became thoughtful as he analysed the bullets.

"That was d-d-disgusting, just like you lot eating grazers! Disgusting!" Fax stumbled his way and sat on a concrete plant pot. He looked at the leader as if to say, "you're beginning to bug me," and with one concentrated blast of air from his lips, the fusilier flew out from the confinement of the Tower of London and into the river Thames.

"Get out! This is my house!" Fax glared at the others. They soon became aware that this was no ordinary man, and everyone evacuated.

Fax pulled down the portcullis as the last fusilier left. There he noticed a white handkerchief being waved and a head peering round the corner; it was the British prime minister.

"It seems everywhere you go, old boy, chaos follows. Can we have a chin wag? A cup of tea?"

Fax smiled and said to leave him alone as he was busy. The prime minister warned that this couldn't be allowed to continue, and he was to give up immediately. Fax just waved him off as the prime minister told him; the world was on its way.

Fax could hear the world was on its way. The American fleet, Chinese navy, Russian army, and Japanese ships were communicating with one another and directing their aircraft carriers, warships, and nuclear subs towards the golden-capped hill.

"Funny that," Fax muttered.

That evening, Fax was nibbling on one of the royal plates when it occurred that he didn't really want to eat the pretty; it was destroying it. He remembered what Kyle said about gold, how there is lots of it in the vaults under the Bank of England. He put the orb and sceptre back in the jewel room and, still crowned, flew to Number Ten and grabbed the prime minister, who amusingly agreed and accompanied Fax to the bank.

The prime minister told the security staff how it was useless to resist and, more than likely, they would die first if they tried to stop Fax. The armed guards kept their guns ready until Fax ripped off the vault's bomb-proof door as if it were made of paper, and within a friendly conversation about family and friends, he melted the inner door. He walked in, eyes boggling, and ate a bar of gold like it was chocolate. He was munching happily when, in a puff of wind, the prime minister saw the power of the Bank of England evaporate before his very eyes.

Back at the Tower of London, Fax had stacked the gold neatly. He calculated that he had enough for the corridors and was so happy that he didn't have to destroy any of the pretty stuff.

Chapter Eight
DRONES

Fax's happiness bound no barriers. His gold power bars were safe, so much so that he sat on the tower's park bench playing Space Invaders. But he could almost feel himself sluggish, as if he had eaten too much golden syrup.

Had he discovered a weakness? If he had, a secret was needed. The supernova indicator was bursting; it was the gold. He couldn't look at another piece and felt he needed to expel a bit before he became critical and exploded.

He tuned to the progress of the military to keep his mind off it, like using an old transistor radio. He understood the Russians were advancing on the English Channel, having submarined through the Barents and North Sea. The Americans were anchored outside Jersey Harbour, having crossed the North Atlantic Ocean, and were waiting. The Chinese came through the Indian Ocean and were currently cruising up the Atlantic. But one thing Fax understood: the world's army was going to converge on the golden-capped hill all at the same time.

Fax stood up, farted, and within a second found himself stuck on Mars.

"Bloody hell," he muttered and melted his way out with his eye laser. Water was automatically detected. "You could bring this back to life," he muttered and darted back to Earth.

He landed in a cow pat and walked to the summit of the golden-capped hill. At the top, he stood with the sceptre in his left hand, orb in his right hand, and the crown on his head, like a king guarding his realm. He looked out over the tranquil blue. The birds were tweeting, and the breeze was a respectable twenty degrees. Fumes started to blur the two blues of the horizon as the devilment of the diesel directed those propellers. It wasn't long before reconnaissance planes flew overhead with pilots confirming his position.

Admiral Barratry, leader of the American fleet, puffed on a fat cigar as he challenged his Chinese counterpart to a race to see whom could destroy Fax first.

This was childish behaviour, as far as Fax was concerned, lighting the barbeque he had brought with him. He mindlessly watched and listened to people chatting over the airwaves. Suddenly, he thought to break the mundane, and he phoned Kyle, who was watching the 24-hour coverage of the invasion of "The Fax."

"Hello, baby," Fax said cheekily.

"You're quite the mad one, aren't you? I thought you wanted to keep a low profile."

"Me mad? Yes. Well, we will see."

"The Americans have sent a fleet; that's eight warships!" Kyle snapped. "An aircraft carrier, twenty-four planes and eight Apache gunships. The Chinese sent the same, and the Russians sent six nuclear submarines. Not to say that every country is on military alert, except for this country, oddly, as our prime minister thinks you're great! Did you tell every world leader you were going to scrap them if they didn't do what you asked?"

"Think Bertie fancies me? Yep, probably. Childish behaviour?" Fax looked at his memory file. "Oh yes, when I told him my plans, the North Korean leader got most excited and started humping my leg. The Russian said, 'Do you realise we drink vodka in this country, and we don't scare easy?' But then he apologised as I showed him a handful of wires that I pulled out from under his desk.

"The Chinese bowed as he referred to the container ship. The American sat in his chair, overwhelmed that I caught him playing solitaire and wondering how the hell I got past his guards. The Austrian asked if I wanted a barbecue! The Canadian, well, she was lovely! The Brazilian was quite adamant that the country was his to do with what he liked, for which I gave him the reptilian eye. He then sat down and asked if I wanted a tequila!"

"Sounds like you're having a whale of a time then," Kyle responded. "Are you sure you're not the one being childish?"

"Yes, well, I'm sixty-six million years old!" both Fax and Kyle said at the same time.

"There is lots to do. I've powered up the Pantominuim with ten tonnes of gold—it's nearly full. Places to go people to see."

"Pantominuim?" Kyle asked, puzzled. "On the news they said you stole the crown jewels and England's gold reserve?"

"Yes, well there is lots to do," Fax repeated. "You call them drones; the Pantominuim is like an orchestra to get things done. The darkness is coming, but don't be scared." Fax giggled, ending the conversation.

Fax was aware that war was pointing his way, as "just blow him up and be done with it" had been discussed.

Suddenly, Apache gunships rose up the cliff face and were facing him. Through a speaker, Fax was told to surrender or be destroyed. Fax waved and continued to eat the nuts he had roasted. The order was given to fire one missile. Fax caught it and threw it at the moon, startling the army.

Fax had been nibbling just enough gold to keep himself topped up; he wasn't going to overindulge again. He could feel the sweats coming but just about kept them at bay. He started to blow sarcastically, as if out of breath, and put his hand up as if to stay a break was needed. The helicopters caught everything and relayed directly to the aircraft carriers.

A cannon was made ready. Fax understood it would more than likely take out the entire golden-capped hill. He sent a signal to Pantominuim, and a drone fired out from a porthole from under the sea and sped through the ocean like a torpedo. It propelled itself from the ocean and embedded itself inside the muzzle of the cannon, melting it.

In the meantime, as the army was reloading, Fax directed drones to block every cannon, gun muzzle, and exhaust pipe. The nuclear subs and aircraft carriers had their propellors snapped off, and anchors were put on the decks as conversation entered into chaos. The aircraft carriers, warships and submarines fell dead and floated with the tide. Fax bowed with elegance, did a little twirl, and signalled that all was not over yet.

The drones swarmed out from hundreds of portholes along the Jurassic coast faster than a gatling gun. The silver balls transformed into house-sized fighter drones that caught each helicopter and aircraft like prey in flight. The submarines were harpooned like whales, then raised from the ocean, dripping. It took twenty fighter drones and eighty workers to fly these, the same for the aircraft carriers, but slightly less for the warships. Together with the crew aboard, the drones flew west.

Fax had no time. His sensors notified him of an incoming nuclear warhead. It was launched from Russia, and it was unmistakably coming to the south coast of Britain. Fax blasted a golden laser with data into the receiver on the moon and messaged two fighter drones to intercept the launched nuclear missile.

He needed to rid the planet of weapons that could destroy her, and he had details of their locations in his quantum. He linked with the drone Pantominuim to dispose of them. Ten fighters, together with a hundred worker drones, were sent out per bomb. Fax watched as the launch capabilities of each were being deleted from his database. He wanted it to be as if they never existed, so he programmed for their infrastructure to be ripped out also. The bombs he sent to the moon, and the metal infrastructure went west.

The phone rang. "Hello, PM," Fax answered.

"Fax, you beautiful Troodon, you stopped that bloody bomb."

"I've stopped you all now, you crazy dumb fucks!" Fax swore.

"We all send our gratitude. If nobody has them, nobody will want them," reassured the British prime minister. "Why, are your drones going west? To Yellowstone?"

"Seems natural!"

Fax was aware of the 6,839 nuclear devices due to head for the moon. He had a plan, but he wasn't quite sure it could be done, having tried it once before. The moon drones would take the nukes from the Jurassic drones and then would return to the Pantominuim!

***

At Yellowstone, Fax hid his arrival and sat where Arizona and Strawberry first spotted the container ship. It wasn't long before a question popped into his quantum. It was about the people aboard the ships, and it came from that pesky conscience.

Fax flew down through the trees, fumbled out of the bushes and transformed, appearing as Kyle dressed as a hiker. Strawberry heard the commotion and asked Kyle-o-Fax about life, the universe, and the stars, to which Kyle-o-Fax replied "yeah" to all.

"I hear there are more ships coming, and they have their crews aboard," commented Kyle-o-Fax

"Crews aboard! More ships," replied Strawberry, edging for how he knew this.

"It's on the internet. Look." Kyle-o-Fax showed her the live footage.

"Coming here? They will die if they land like the containership."

"The container ship was unmanned; I don't think they will land the same way, as the drones are being very careful, don't you think?" Kyle-o-Fax indicated.

"Yeah, we should have a massive party, could have hotdog stands, burger bars, beer, a festival," Strawberry joked.

Then, to Strawberry's surprise, Kyle-o-Fax passed her a bar of gold and said, "Good idea! Get some tents and marquees—and invite your friends. Also get sleeping bags, bottles of water and anything else you think people will need. I think you have a couple of days. I will be back later; keep the change. I'll bring you ten gold bars when it is all over." Fax thought about the motivation of offered money.

"How much is this worth?" Strawberry asked, holding the bar.

"Haven't a clue. It weighs four hundred ounces, maybe one million dollars. Bye."

Kyle-o-Fax disappeared back into the bushes while Strawberry beamed in happy disbelief. She showed Arizona, and he danced around too. They both told the rangers, and they too joined in the dance. After that, they were careful to whom they showed it. They all organised a party of special significance; there were flyers, and bunting covered in the words "Everyone is Welcome at Yellowstone."

***

Back in sunny old England, it was mostly curiosity that stirred people's imaginations, as children and parents alike were pointing in wonderment at the harpooned metal hulks that passed over their towns and cities. Firstly, in southern England, people waved in Charmouth and through Axminster. Over the black-down hills, sheep peered with one eye, then round over with their legs in the air. In Wellington, men cursed and shook their walking sticks. The drones touched the coast at Porlock and leapt out over the Bristol Channel at Lynton. There were tears in Tenby, a dance in Dale, Whiskey in Wexford, and Guinness in Galway. They crossed the Atlantic until Newfoundland gave them a firework salute. Then, Nova Scotia folk waved and went happily berserk. The military staff donned Hawaiian shirts and danced to the Bee Gees on the decks of the ships. The president of the United States was aware of the carnival and watched live footage with welcoming but slightly worried delight. He was more concerned at the swarm of drones emptying the military bases from the West Coast.

Ajax Tavern and her cameraman were capturing tanks, jeeps, missile launchers and military equipment falling from the sky that was covering Old Faithful at Yellowstone.

***

A phone rang at the White House. The president, picking it up, immediately guessed who it was.

"Fax?"

"No, it's David Attenborough!"

"Bertie tells me you are a reptilian who is named Fax."

"Bertie, ha, I swear he fancies me! Ha, bless the British prime minster. Okay, Fax it is."

"I like what you have done with the nukes. My sources tell me they can't find any evidence of their existence."

"Hopefully disappearing from memory with every second president!" snapped Fax.

"They say you put them on the moon and that you have drones up there too?"

"Yes, there are six thousand eight hundred and thirty-nine nuclear devices at the moment."

"Won't that pollute space?"

"Space is radiation; there are very few places in the universe that aren't. The surface of the Earth is one place you don't want radiation."

"Yes, we're not the brightest. Anyway, what's the plan, man?" asked the American president.

"I'm sending a drone. Pack a bag and wear something happy. Everything else will be provided. See you soon."

"Fax, are there are more of you?"

"Trillions alive and some biologically detached. It's complicated!" Fax raised an eyebrow.

The president donned a Hawaiian shirt, shorts, and sandals and stepped inside the Cadillac that had landed on the White House lawn. The drone transformed into something more aerodynamic and silently headed toward the sky carnival. The president landed on the lead aircraft carrier as it hovered over Central Park in New York. There were cheers and laughter from the residents below before they sped towards their final destination.

At Yellowstone, bands played to welcome military personnel. The Russian and Chinese presidents were both flown in. Their drones turned into burger bars, and each leader welcomed their countrymen with plant burgers, plant dogs and fizz. It was a very organised affair, like an airport. The nuclear-powered submarines and aircraft carriers used drones like buses to ferry their staff.

The odd tank, plane and helicopter landed in a populated area, much to shock of the personnel who climbed out. The drones then lifted the diesel-powered war machines into the many queues that gathered high in the sky at the west end of the caldera ready for the drop. Fax programmed the drones to remove the nuclear fuel from the submarines and aircraft carriers and to throw them at the moon.

Arizona, Strawberry, and friends were buzzing around building campfires and laying out sleeping arrangements for the thousands of military staff, who for one night only could party until dawn, as there seemed to be a growing anxiety.

Chapter Nine
CORRIDORS

The military staff were all happy to be back on terra firma and alcoholically drank their way to a merry night. Campfires were lit and music played, but anxiety was airborne at Yellowstone. It was as if something was saying, "Party by all means, but don't stay to long."

Fax was amused by this; instincts shouldn't be a part of his quantum makeup. It was something he understood that would be lost when a biological being was morphed into an infinite, but somehow he sensed it too.

He couldn't tell where it came from. He had run diagnostics many times before, and they always pointed to a blank spot in his quantum, a kind of cave where vast data seemed to be stored but he couldn't gain access. It could as easily be empty or full of bats. All he knew was that it was vast, and he missed it somehow. It was probably the part of his brain that kept him alive, or maybe life was trying to claw its way back into his quantum. Whatever it was, he thought, it was intriguing!

He messaged his lunar drones and arrived back at the tower, where he started polishing his jewels. Crowds gathered outside. People were mostly in support of Fax, as many were cheering and hooraying outside the walls of the tower, but obviously there were some who booed and hissed also. It was funny, as the negativity mostly came from the smartly dressed suits.

Fax caressed his jewels with marvel and delight as a million or so thoughts a second were going on in his mind. It was kind of relaxing being so occupied and not aware of any outside disturbance. He was almost done composing the operational orchestra for the drones to complete the corridors, but it was complicated.

Then, all of a sudden, there came a little bumbling, squawking noise from the front gate. It was British Prime Minister Bertie again, thumbling about and chatting to himself. Fax stopped the program and smiled, as he did like the eccentric human. He reminded him of the professor, as clever men do tend to behave funny at times. But with Bertie, he must the cleverest of them all!

Fax peeped through the portcullis.

"Ha! There you are, old boy. Bloody sterling work, if I don't say so myself."

Fax cursed slightly, as obviously he had peeped too hard.

"Now about these wildlife corridors, yes? Had the French prime minister on the line—lovely chap, always brings me garlic. I haven't quite got my head around it. Same with the German mind you, always brings me sausage. I think one is to ward off vampires, the other is to bloody well club the vampires around the head with. Crazy stuff, don't you think, old boy? What are they all about, you know, the corridors?"

Fax looked bemused and lifted the portcullis, nodding Bertie in. "I see you still have handguns," Fax muttered.

"You can't deny me a little protection, can you, Faxy?"

"Protection from who? The old lady or the young baby who were innocently born into this gasoline-stinking world?"

"You like it here?" asked Bertie while adjusting his toupee, sniffing and letting loose his massive teeth as he smiled.

"Believe me, I was woken by something bigger than you or me," Fax replied, "It's a bit of a holiday from the norm, I suppose!"

"What's the norm?"

Fax looked as though the conversation was pointless. "Well . . . it's like your dreams, except I can choose the dream. As far as I'm concerned, this could be a dream, so I could rip your head off and it wouldn't make any difference."

"That would leave an awful mess on the cobbles," Bertie said with a smile.

"The Tower of London has seen it many times before."

"That's history, old boy, history."

"History or program, it's a bit boring, and I didn't choose it myself. Never before have I been told what conscience to live!"

"Boring? You've stolen the crown jewels, and you live in the Tower of London. How can you call it boring?"

"Kill count too low. I've lived through wars that lasted thousands of years. It seems that here I am conscious of conscience; I even got a touch of morality!"

"Not a bad thing, old boy!"

"It's simply not me." Fax looked worried for himself.

"Well, anyway, as I was saying, old boy, the French, German, Russian, Canadian, and multiple other leaders condemn your proposed wildlife corridors."

Fax looked thoughtful. "Hmm . . . proposed means planned, a suggestion, or something for consideration. There was nothing proposed; it simply is. From John O' Groats to Land's End, from North Carolina on the East Coast to California on the West, from Nova Scotia to Alaska, from Mexico to the southern tip of Argentina, from Portugal to the Bering Sea, through China, India, Pakistan, Afghanistan, Iran, Africa and Australia, to name just a few."

"What about the people?" moaned Bertie.

"You're the people, Bertie. I am the Earth or," Fax paused, "shall I say it's just the start. You should relax." Fax smiled. "Three mornings from now, you will wake up to a brighter world!"

***

Two days later

Fax was hovering at eighty kilometres, touching space with his little toe. He was watching the Earth spin, and as the sun set on the Bering Strait, it seemed the logical place to start. Fax waved forward his first of many divisions. It was comprised of one hundred billion drone workers programmed to dismantle.

Absolute darkness was the first part of his orchestration, so that nobody could see what was going on. The thought was simple; just switch off the generators that lit the lights, powered the televisions, and boiled the kettles.

But no, Fax had other plans. He instructed the dismantlers to rip out the furnaces that boiled the water, that created the steam, that turned the turbines, that lit up the lights, that powered televisions, and boiled the kettles. And so they did.

Behind the dismantlers raced the medical transporters that silently gassed their way through the landscape, picking up the fallen as they went.

Old Mrs Aroha Maori from a little town call Matawai in North Island, New Zealand had been muttering on her porch for days since the chisel-faced government man came. "There is no way I'm moving. Bloody government telling me what to do, do they know I'm almost ninety?" She told him about Ashley, her pet goldfish, and showed him Shelly, her shotgun, and said that if she was made to move, she wasn't going to throw the fish at him, as she smiled with Shelly in her arms.

The night of the drone-tilla, she again sat on her porch in her comfiest of chairs. The evening was summer warm, and a little light kept her company. Suddenly, she questioned if she had fallen blind; she blinked, as everything was in complete darkness. Her blindness was unmistaken, and the feeling of sudden sleep was for sure death, only to wake the next day in a field, on some grass that she didn't recognise.

"Bloody fish!" she muttered. Ashley was looking at her. "Where's my bloody house gone? They took my house and my poor Shelly!"

She looked out over a newly planted area with young and old trees that stretched out across the landscape for what seemed like forever. There wasn't a house or road to be seen.

"Would you like a cup of tea?" came a voice from behind her.

She turned her stiff neck and placed her glasses over her eyes. She focused, only to see thousands of people sleeping or sitting in shock, as they had also been picked up in the night and placed there.

"Cup of tea would be nice. Here, young one!"

"My name is Mary, ma'am."

"I don't care if your name is the grim reaper herself," she grouched. "Put a drop of whiskey in there. Now, there's a good girl."

It was the same all over the world. The ten-kilometre-wide wildlife corridors void of anything man-made was creating havoc. Fax, to rub salt in the wound, also erected DNA fences to stop any human interference.

***

That morning, Fax was relaxing in reality. He was back at the Tower of London, sitting on the stone seating arrangement like the kind Henry the Eighth sat on, and charging in the sun. Everything was going well until he heard those immortal words again.

"Hello, Faxy!" said the tombstones. "Not at all happy, Faxy old boy. The country has come to a complete standstill. Not used to the mundane us English. You know it's beyond?"

"Your lights are on? Are they not?"

"Yes, but how? There is no coal, gas or nuclear, but we have steam Fax, we have steam!" He clapped.

"I've sacrificed one of my fighter drones for each one of your furnaces. There will be no burning anymore; it's childish and irresponsible. The fighter drones will glow red hot for fifty years. As long as you feed them, your water will boil and your turbines will turn. Gold is the key! Gold is the key to everything!" Fax looked dreamlike.

"The country is at a standstill. We can't pass the corridor."

Fax smiled. "That's the whole point."

"People will die."

"Ten percent, that's all that is needed! Ten percent of your brightest," Fax muttered.

"People are still wondering what they are to do."

"Some of my drones have converted themselves into houses and hotels. You need to plant trees, Prime Minister. Or shall I call you Bertie?"

"We all have to be gardeners?"

"Basically, yes!" With that, Fax took hold of the British prime minister's arm. "Hold on tight."

Bertie closed his eyes like a school kid being forced on to his first ride at the fair. Fax flew up and out over London. Bertie opened one eye then the other. He started to smile, as he felt safe in Fax's hands.

"I contacted the press a while ago," Fax explained. "We are going to the most evident place of your injustice." Below, a great grey path stretched out before them.

"That's the M-Four," pointed out Bertie.

"M-One to the M-Ninety, miss a few. All boil my piss! I prefer it when you used horse and cart!"

"The doesn't say much for progress," pointed out Bertie.

"Your progress is fuelling your destruction. It doesn't exist. But someone like you? There be bats in my belfry! I tell thee! I tell thee!"

"There be bats in my belfry too!" Bertie replied, squeezing Fax tight with a comforting smile.

From height they could see all the roads, train tracks, farms and lines ending at the giant brownish-green snake that stretched up and down the county into a smoggy disappearance.

Fax started to descend. Bertie was puzzled, as the grey line of the M4 didn't end as bluntly as he was led to believe. Instead, it had a bulbous, blurry ending. They landed; the giant ghostly dome as large as a football stadium was before them. Bertie's mind was doing summersaults, and he stood ogling. Fax wasn't so interested, but he did make a tutting sound at his disapproval that it wasn't already finished. The noise was deafening.

Cars and press vans were approaching in the distance. "Now, Bertie," Fax said to get his attention, "remembering that you're the British prime minister, I hope you don't embarrass me! Act as though you know exactly what is going on." Fax rounded his eyes. "And do your bloody fly up!"

Suddenly, the whizzing and pooping started to ramp down. There were a few hisses as great volumes of air seemed to be released as the dome slowly started to shrink into an igloo type of shape. It came a halt and a great door opened. It revealed the eight lanes of the motorway dropping down into a vast tunnel system. Fax grabbed Bertie's arm and started to walk towards it. They noticed a ribbon spanning the entire length of the entrance to the tunnel.

"That's for you." Fax pointed and flew into the tunnel.

A couple of minutes later, he appeared next to Bertie. "All is well. Bloody marvellous, roads marked, lights on and ready to go. Oh yes, and you can cut the ribbon at the other end!" Fax sneaked Bertie a pair of scissors.

The press gathered and the prime minister cut the tape. "The M-Four nature corridor underpass is open!"

Fax walked into what was housed under the dome, and Bertie flagged down a BBC news crew and got a lift through the tunnel.

It was like Park Street. Fax compared his internal image. Everything was unnamed, it just needed people. There was a tourist information centre displaying everything about the wildlife corridor and how folks can help. There were lists of all the mosses, trees, and flowers, but most important was the mighty earthworm.

The worker drones had names, and a story was told about how they took the elements of the earth and made the tunnels possible. Also stated was that the need for the nature corridors was due to the haste in the development of the motorcar, as in its development people had no regard for nature.

The car was invented because of the massive piles of horse shit in the city of New York. There was information on how petrol took the place of the electric car. There were lists of inventors that feared horses. There were lists of inventors who were lazy and couldn't be bothered to walk anywhere. The invention of the motorcar conjured the tanks and fighting machines, and that was why—or one reason— they had been disposed of.

"You see," Fax said as Bertie stood beside him, "no predicament, old boy. You get to drive to Bath and Bristol after all. Heavens forbid you have to walk!"

"I do think the world could do with your tunnels," commented Bertie.

"Well, no doubt the press has beamed pictures around the world by now."

The British prime minister's telephone started to ring.

"Hello, Bertie, it's Bucks A Million. The president wants a word."

"Morning, Bertie. Fax, I assume?" The president of the United Stated sounded upbeat. "Obviously, every country wants to know the same thing. How the hell did he put ten kilometres of tunnel in overnight?"

"He's got these factory-type construction drones I've never seen the likes of. Apparently, he had two spare and thought it would be a good idea!"

"Ajax Tavern at ABC news has told me that power stations are now falling from the sky at Yellowstone, and the caldera is nearly full!"

"Well, Tex, not quite sure we have seen the last of that. Fax has no love of guns and has called us lazy bar stewards when it comes to our use of cars! It's some of his fighter drones that are producing our electricity, just as long as we feed them gold!" Bertie noted.

"Gold, he loves his gold. We are still in darkness over here, battery light only. Hopefully, the nation will wake up with the power on. France, Germany and Russia are saying they experienced power loss overnight."

"Tell Fax to come and see me in person. We have lots to discuss."

Fax looked at Bertie with cheeky eyes.

"I will ask Fax, but I don't think there will be any telling him."

"Ask him then. Is there no negotiation? What's he up to next? His power is worrying."

Fax smiled as the conversation ended. "Obviously, I'm taking a vacation afterwards!"

"Our royals just sent a text. You can keep the jewels. They somewhat approve of your efforts," Bertie said with a smile.

Fax smiled and pointed to the crown still on his head and said, "Pretty!"

Chapter Ten
THE WHALERS

Fax dropped Bertie back at 10 Downing Street and popped over to the White House. The Secret Service made the president aware that Fax was sitting at his desk, so he looked in the mirror and adjusted his tie before he went in.

"Tex, my old mate, how's it hanging?" Fax asked with a smile.

The president stared. "You're green?"

"Green as the grass. Your observational skills are tremendous! But I'm handsome with it!" Fax replied.

The president lifted an eyebrow. "Power is restored?"

"Power is just finishing off on the West Coast; it's been a busy night!"

"Bit of an understatement that!"

"Could be. You summoned me?" Fax said as he put on the president's glasses and peered over the lenses. "Wow, wow, wow. Before you say anything, I've already spoken to your other leaders. Yes, I've completed the corridors. Yes, I have bridged every natural waterway. Yes, I have dumped your combustion power stations. If you leave a bar of twenty-four carat gold at each road you want tunnelled, it will be done."

"A bar of gold?" The president lifted an eyebrow again.

"There is always a cost, Tex, you understand. It matters not to me."

"What's next? Bertie said something about guns and cars?"

Fax looked as though Bertie had grassed him up. "Well, all I know is that since my rude awakening from under the golden-capped hill, I haven't had a lot of . . . me time. So, I plan on a little holiday, or vacation in your case. I don't know what's next. All I know is that something is coming."

"Something? What!" The president looked shocked.

Fax then shook the president's hand. "I'm sure everything we be alright. After all, has anyone died?" He giggled. Fax then opened the window and flew out.

That night, Fax had the tunnels completed, and the nature corridors were making perfect sense worldwide. The president was a little cross, though, as he had been looking everywhere, but he was going to have to explain to his wife why he had lost his wedding ring!

Fax alerted Kyle he was coming to pay him a visit. Fax spotted the university from space and fell towards green but landed as the cheekboned human. Kyle was in his usual place, and old cheekbones called up the timber stairs for him to come down.

"You're him again!" Kyle blurted.

"Yes, well, you know, got to blend in and all that. Fax is bigger than any nature-loving rock star. Where's the professor? Have we thought younger recently, or does he still like a good flushing?"

Kyle ran back up to his office, closed everything down, spoke to the chancellor via telephone, and booked unpaid leave, as there was no chance that he was going to miss out this time.

They walked through the university, passing red-velvet-draped windows and the odd apple core.

"I do like the look. It's like your cool but also dark," Kyle commented.

"There are infinite DNA combinations, and I could project a unique person at any time. Like so!"

"Jesus," remarked Kyle as they entered great hall.

"No, Sean Connery," pointed out Fax. "I'm only playing."

"What do you think?" Fax stood as Rambo.

"What do you think?" Fax stood as Indiana Jones.

"What do you think?" Fax stood as John McCain.

"What do you think?" Fax stood as Luke Skywalker.

"What do you think?" Fax stood as the Terminator.

"What do you think?" Fax stood as Tom Jones.

"Where have you got these images from?" asked Kyle.

"Films, obviously!"

"Ok, Cheekbones will do," Kyle said, looking amused.

"Christ, we've had it now," the professor muttered as he snuck up behind them.

"Right, you two, I need some me time! I'm thinking about a little road trip, and you are accompanying me, okay?" Fax looked as if it was needed.

"Field trip, we love a good field trip, don't we, Kyle? Especially when billionaires pay. The name is Professor Woodrow Malarky. You can probably tell I'm up for a bit of fun," he replied confidently. "I will have to cancel with Burt and Sid. Poker night," he added thoughtfully.

They both made the arrangements and jumped into the limousine.

"Where are we going?" the professor asked.

"Africa, maybe."

"Africa! I thought we were going to Seatown."

"I want to see my home environment," Fax said.

"Why not fly? You can fly!"

"I would be there and back again. Then what will I have to do? I must wait, as someone, somewhere is going to give me my next orders."

"Orders? Who gives you orders?" Kyle smirked.

"Both of you need to understand that there is a bigger picture here at play, and anyway—one way or the other—we all take orders; it's normal."

The radio was on in the background, and as the professor followed signs for the channel crossing, Fax listened intently between conversations. Music was something Fax could waste time listening to, as it conjured up feelings.

"Obviously, being Troodon, I am far superior to you humans!"
Both eyebrows raised. "But there is something I'm jealous of! Bloody
foot tappers I called you. I must have heard you thousands of years
ago. Your mother's heartbeat, that's where your creation of music
derived from. No wonder I can't hum a bloody tune; there was no big
blood pumper in my eggshell!"

"Right." The professor hadn't thought of that before. "That's
good, Fax. But we need to ditch the limo. I am not getting a bloody
ferry in this."

They gave the limo to a homeless family, and Kyle bought an
electric Land Cruiser. Kyle smiled as he clocked Fax trying to tap his
foot.

They were boarding the ferry when a news flash came on the
radio. The broadcast spoke of the pointless killing of whales in the
Antarctic Basin. The newscaster went on to say that, although 99 per
cent of the Earth's population was against such cruelty, the people
were powerless to act—except for Greenpeace.

Fax got out of the car and told them both he would be back by
the time they reached France. He darted at nearly a hundred thousand
kilometres per hour toward the broadcasted destination. From the air,
he spotted eight whaling vessels and plunge-dived like a seabird into
the water. He propelled himself through the sea and flung himself
onto the factory ship that was spearheading the hunt. The crew was
absolutely mortified as they looked on. There on the ship's bow, at
fifteen-foot tall, smoking a two-foot-long cigar, wearing a Greenpeace
bandana and holding the G gun in his right flipper, stood a killer whale.

"Hey, boys, my name is Orca, and I am a killer whale," he said in
a deep, menacing way.

The crew looked stunned, as before them was the nightmare
that haunted their wildest dreams: a whale that could defend itself.
Three fainted as the cheesy black-and-white grin, in which Fax had
purposely included larger teeth, beamed with glee.

"What we got here, boys?" Orca raged on, pointing to a minke
whale that was dead on the deck, with the guts removed.

The crew fled below deck, leaving behind the one crew member that was manning the grenade-tipped harpoon. The harpoon spun round as the captain came from his quarters to see what the commotion was all about. He retreated in disbelief and went to the armoury to hand out shotguns and AK-47s to the willing.

Orca warned them that the attack would be futile and stated that this was just penance for the atrocity they had unleashed upon his cousins. Orca was engulfed in flames and peppered with small-arms fire as the harpoon was released. The crew looked on in desperation as the smoke eased to see if he was down.

Orca grinned. "Is that all you got, boys?"

With that, the handheld genocide gun was set to stun, and an electromagnetic pulse rendered the ship useless while knocking out the remainder of the crew. He thought about throwing them overboard and treating them as they had treated others, but to kill seemed to be beyond his mind. *Hurt, yes; humiliate, of course; torture, maybe; but not kill.* Orca returned the compliment to six other vessels, leaving one for the spiritual voyage home. He told them that if they ever stopped seeking forgiveness, he would sink the ship and tell the sharks.

By this time, the people on the Greenpeace vessel were applauding, but the iceberg and fleet spotter who caught a glimpse of Orca in his telescope wasn't so exuberant, as he cursed the sea and went to have a lie down. The steam blowers engulfed the ocean with their titanic sound. Fax, who appeared to them as egg born, stood on the manned whaling ship and bowed to the closing Greenpeace vessel. He sneaked a bit of a gold. Then, one by one, drones rose out of the ocean and flew the whaling ships north to be dropped in the middle of Yellowstone Park.

***

"I'm back," Fax said, walking up the pair in the restaurant.

"Where have you been?" Woodrow asked. "It's been almost an hour."

"Just went for a dump, you know," Fax said smugly. "You lot put a price on everything. This money thing?" Fax paused. "Imagine putting a price on every human head and knowing you are being hunted! This money thing might see my wrath after all!"

Fax fell into silence and walked off. He donned sunglasses and mingled free for a while, people-watching. He found himself on the bow of the ferry reminiscing over lost and past times, when a flashing of fire entered his vision. He felt as if the boundaries of his quantum were being tested once again. He looked at his astronomical clock; the hour was young, but the time seemed late. It couldn't be Goat, as if he had any inclination that he was awake, he would already be here.

What could it be? Fax scanned and scanned.

"There you are, Fax," came voices that had a calming effect

Fax followed Kyle into the casino, where he watched him place a number of chips on the table as a wheel spun. He looked at the speed of the wheel and the circulating ball and moved all of Kyle's chips to number 19. Kyle looked at him, smiled, and watched as the ball landed on four black. Fax winked at Kyle, as it was close.

Kyle handed Fax a £20 chip. He waited for the wheel to spin and the ball to be tossed. This time he placed the chip on 28, and Kyle was shuffled £720. Fax again watched the wheel, and after a bit of quiet calculation, he put the lot on zero. The ball bounced around and, to the joy of the pair of them, they gained £26,640. This seemed unfavourable with the management, and they were quietly asked to leave.

The ferry docked in Calais, and they were off. The traffic was quiet, but the professor thought they would probably hit Paris at rush hour, as he knew the route well. He had spent several summers in the south camping and caravanning when his family was young. Nowadays, his children had children of their own, and his son Travis was living in Florida, while his daughter Megan was studying in Edinburgh. She wanted to be like her father, the professor explained.

Fax was once again drifting in and out. He simulated walking on the methane moon of Titian, thinking about the Infinite Time

Consortium. He needed time but was puzzled as to why on one hand he thought he had all the time in the world and on the other time had already run out. He didn't want Razor, Jude, Cormac, and especially Goat to start pulling the strings, as he knew they weren't as forgiving as him. Dolly would be alright, though, and he was looking forward to their conversation.

Paris was behind them, and Fax noticed birds flying in the partly clouded sky with one eye and with the other eye was scanning the moon drones. He was going to have to visit the moon sometime; just to make sure the nuclear bombs were safe. Eventually he was going to have them transported to Mars as he was making plans to use them to ignite the core so creating a magnetic field like the planet once had.

But for now a little rest and relaxation was the plan so he summoned a little temporary fancy. Data appeared to him in his quantum. It read: "A date with Nadinska, a roko dancer from the Echoes of Ecstasy nightclub. It was on a planet orbiting a star called Discanti, where the magnetic storms were so enchanting."

Virtually, Fax was enthralled as the world slipped past the window. He understood the wind was upon his face and thought how he missed breathing. His brain brought the radio to the front of his mind; it was soothing and saved him from any overexcited thought production. He leaned back in the car, listening, until he began to hear voices. Then there were more voices and singing. Drums were banging, the bass was booming, guitars were screeching, pianos were pinging, trumpets were blowing, and violins were skidding. There was layer upon layer of music and voices scrambling in his head. Fax lay motionless, going translucent. Kyle noticed there was something wrong and asked Woodrow to pull over. They both looked in the back, but Fax was gone. All that was left was his diamond core on the back seat. They looked at each other, and both went to grab it.

This time their touch didn't bring Fax back.

"What do we do now?" Puzzled Kyle.

The professor was studying Fax's diamond core to see if there were any buttons or triggering devices.

"Fax mentioned something about virtual reality being where he has spent the last sixty or so million years. He has probably gone to see some old friends or something," Kyle said on a positive note.

"Surly he would have said something. We haven't known him for that long, but he seems a reasonable chap." Woodrow tried to move the diamond again.

"That's about right, 'Sympathy for the Devil,'" Fax said as he stuck his head between the two front seats, shaking it.

"Where did you go?" asked the professor.

"Christ, man, this planet is noisy. Just turn it up a little so I can take a datum off this frequency. That's better," Fax said.

"Why? What's wrong?" the professor asked.

"Nothing really. I wanted to listen to what this planet was saying, and I had every radio station in my head going off all at the same time. It froze me."

"News flash," the radio announcer said, "the American government has said it was Fax who dumped the whaling fleet that had been hunting whales in the oceans in and around the Antarctic Basin into the middle of Yellowstone Park."

"Brilliant! That's always made my blood boil," Kyle cheered.

"My son asked me when he was young if people are still killing the blue whales. He said it was the biggest animal and it was wrong for us to kill it. A tear did come to my eye that day, as I had to lie—but no more!" the professor cheered.

They all cheered, even Fax, who was looking a little sheepish. Then they noticed people laughing in their cars, and horns started honking.

"It seems, at last, somebody cares about the world. Fax, we love you! This is Trevor Tailor, BBC News."

Chapter Eleven

THE NIGHTMARE AND THE HONEYBEE

Kyle puckered up his lips and blew Fax a big kiss as he stood by the car listening to the depleting car horns going up the road. Fax smiled, as he thought the fuss was something to do about nothing, and he was happy to help.

But something was slowly sucking away at his soul, and Fax knew it. It started to plague him like a broken toe, and it was capable of getting him angry, as it was dull, grey and lifeless. It stank of an ancient carbon that had no right to be released. To rub salt into his wounds, his internal quantum notified that one of the wheel bearings had a slightly more elevated temperature as he travelled along.

Fax, his face sullen, lent back in his seat and strained an effort to bypass the obvious and thought about living as a bowling ball for a while, seeing as he never played. It could be fun being chucked down an ally. But after a couple of throws he found with dizziness came a side effect and decided to change his current mini vacation. So, he fed himself into a wood mill, as the blades looked particularly painful, but much to his disappointment, the blades simply shattered. His resolve was to walk into a car filling station, pour petrol over his head and light a match. The explosion was invigorating, and calculated petrol flame had a peculiar oily texture. He walked from the garage onto an alien beach, where he flung himself into an alien sea, so dousing the flame and drowned himself. But still, the sterile grey thing they were travelling on came to the foreground of his quantum, making him drool at the possibly of digging them all up, like the corridors, and returning the land to how it once was, but this seemed like something he wasn't allowed to action.

Kyle had never seen Fax look so sad.

But all is not lost, Fax thought to himself. *No, you are right. I've got to stay focused. Yes, the next time I see one, I'm going to feed myself to a great white. Why wait?* The thought came crashing into his mind. *Yes, why wait indeed?*

Fax's eyes became devious as he flicked through his naughty files, the kind of tales with no happy ending. It didn't take him long before he found one: *Buried Alive.* He looked at the small print, it read: "A land breathier buried alive! Dangerous! The highest virtual setting so to be fully immersed in the experience, and *death* is *inevitable!*"

But Fax thought he didn't have time to die. The last time he virtually died he was reincarnated as a slug, and it took over ten thousand years for him to recover. He was intrigued, though, to actually feel the soil being dropped upon him, choking, suffocating, blinding his eyes. *Could I take the stress,* he asked himself, *and return to reality unscathed? How long would I be buried?* Questions, questions, questions. He banged his head on the window and started chewing at his finger.

Are you all right, Fax? The thought waved in the forefront of his quantum as reality-Fax virtually put his head on a golf tee.

"All right? Do I look all right?!" he said to his virtual good self as sweat began pouring from his brow. "Have you seen what it is like out there? Well, crackers," said Fax to his good self.

I like crackers, responded his good self.

"Well, you would. I would rather chuck myself into a black hole than stay here any longer."

It would probably break!

"Break it? Who am I talking to? Break a black hole indeed. I'll feel it, yes, feel myself getting ripped apart atom by atom," said Fax battling with his conscience.

You need to calm down.

"Calm down!" he shouted. "I am bloody calm! It's just . . . where is the intimacy, the self-governing freedom? Freedom!" Shivered his soul. "Reality is so boring and being bloody sober is a load of crap. Why am I here? What does a Troodon have to do when you got a million or so beautiful ladies asking you for a cuddle?"

Fax could see them beckoning him, enticing him to come and play. Then a jaunt from the car made Fax open his eyes. He immediately knew there were 62,998 hairs on the professor's head, and if he moved he could count the hairs on Kyle's head too.

This could be the most torturous moment I ever endured, he pondered to himself, but then he had another thought. *Could this be my salvation?*

He engaged in conversation. "The wind is coming from the south-westerly direction, and at twenty-eight degrees Celsius, that's about average for a midsummer's day in these parts," he said, so uncomfortable that his virtual self stuck shards of metal through its cheeks.

Kyle and the professor looked at one another, then looked at Fax. The professor raised himself a little for more eye contact in the rearview mirror, but both had the expression of contemplating complexes that weighed far heavier than the bloody weather.

Fax was once again deflated. He experienced the forgotten beachball effect; what he thought was a good idea turned out not to be. He thought it customary to talk about the weather and thought their non-involvement rude.

I could have talked for hours, but now they would rather sit in silence. Should I just talk at them despite their lack of participation? I could tell them about cloud formation, wind circulation, jet streams, hurricanes—but, no, bloody silence, he moaned thoughtfully.

Suddenly, he felt a breeze on his face, one that transported him back to his childhood. It was over in a flash, but he assumed his skin sensors were off. Fax instantly turned from a mountain of boredom into a mouse of inquisitiveness.

This was physical, even very light. It was pain, he thought, and it spooked him, like being covered in spiders. He checked his data core and temporarily shut himself down, then rebooted.

Fax is not Fax if he can feel pain, he thought to himself.

"An indestructible, cursed with feelings," he muttered to his reflection in the window. "It's lucky this wasn't brought to my attention when I swam in the sun."

Then he realised something that wasn't there a moment ago. It was like he wasn't alone. Someone had let themselves in and was roaming about upstairs. There was evidence the cave had opened and shut again. Was it an idea inside his quantum, or was it information they wanted? Fax felt he was being probed and examined. He couldn't fight, negotiate, or refuse. His mind was thinking thoughts he had never thought before. He scanned the entire spectrum of light to see if the glowing dread was hiding elsewhere, but there was nothing. He couldn't pinpoint where it was hiding. So, after a little debate, he chalked it up to a freak occurrence.

The breeze felt almost relaxing. Yet as he wallowed, a lateness occurred to him, as if he was going to miss a special event and visualised alarm bells and sirens of all types.

He wondered if he took too long to return to reality. He needed speed, and lots of it, or his destination would be missed.

By now Paris was in the rearview mirror, and they were on their way to a town called Orleans. The car was still free of conversation, so Fax started to drift. He was peeping into the twilight when he felt as if somebody had pulled the plug to his soul and watched as he disappeared helplessly down the plughole. It became stronger, until he sunk through the back seat of the car and visualised the road racing three centimetres from his eyeballs. Shocked, he gripped the underside of the car like a vice, but as the road whizzed past, his grip waned, and he passed through its hard surface like a bullet through a heartbeat.

He entered a world beyond wind and rain, without a care or a feeling of the present. It was more like a dream within a dream.

What consciousness is this? Fax drearily asked himself. He minded thinking what he thought, but there was no way he wanted to be woken. *A dream—if this is what it is—as I understand it, is the subconscious of the living crossing dimensional plains to experience their other lives. But I'm not alive, so how can this be?*

He drifted deeper and deeper, and felt heavier and heavier as he was further pulled into the depths. His visions churned a hellish red, with rivers of lava racing, twisting, and turning around islands in a devil's sea. He fell further and further, until detail began to fade, and came upon the dense blood-coloured majesty of the metallic. Beyond that was the spinning blackness of a core. Fax wanted to pull the brakes and gaze upon its grandeur, but the stopping didn't start, and he continued to fall through.

He entered a mirror realm where reflected faces were laughing at him. At its heart, where gravity centred at a pinprick, he started to spin, faster and faster until he felt beyond a hurricane and trapped.

This is beyond a joke. After all I have done, where's Bertie when I need him? he thought on realisation.

For some reason, he felt a heart beating, and a brain screaming. The bubble was closing.

"Oh, what's this? Claustrophobia and the air's getting thinner—great!" he shouted.

Never had his invisibility appeared to be so challenged. He looked at his sensors, but there was no evidence that he had ever been found.

Fax was just about to wrestle with a wheelbarrow, when he heard a whisper of a murmur—or was it the sound of a sigh, the heckle of laugher, or the tears that cry? It was something as quiet as a dormouse but as raucous as a stampede. It echoed like water that rippled through his dream.

Fax was delighted that he no longer felt so alone. He started to call, but there was no answer.

He looked at his arms and saw it. He looked at his hands and saw it. His legs, feet, and torso were the same. He pinched his leg; it hurt. So did his side. He pulled his hands in front of his face.

"No wonder I can feel the air getting thinner—I'm alive!" he shouted. He could see veins, and inside there was blood.

Christ, what a feeling!

But the thinness of the air and the tightness of his breath was consuming. Suddenly, it was all a panic, and he started clawing at the walls evermore. His fingers became the hands of the Crackentorp, as did his body, but still his efforts were in vain.

He changed into the Hotham, a creature of the flame, and Fax tried to burn his way out, but all to no avail. Then he changed into the Spartan King, an eight-armed, machine-gun-wielding monster of the Caldercruix star system, who Fax had the utmost respect for, as even he couldn't defeat him on the highest virtual setting. There was no hope. The walls just kept getting tighter and tighter.

Fax needed someone to help. He flew through his virtual characters. He even tried the Hairy Mutt, who was as bold as a coot, but that was the creators for you.

Fax zoomed through his nine hundredth enhanced creature, but still nothing. They were flashing as he was conceding very quickly. Fast approaching was the thousandth, when he paused on the 999th attempt. He thought for a while, then materialised into the Skyrider. Fax held the Skyrider, as he realised his fortunes were about to change. The mind of the confused morphed into a clear version of his formal self, and within the realisation of waking from a nightmare, he opened his eyes.

Kyle was looking at him. "Are you alright?"

"How long have I been out?" Fax asked.

"A good couple of hours. You were twitching like an alcoholic that had just come off the booze." Kyle smiled.

"Never have I felt fear like that!" Fax said pensively.

"Next hotel, we're pulling in. I don't like this stay-up-all-the-time lark," the professor snapped.

"I don't sleep. Something had me!" Fax explained.

"Yes, something had you—sleep," Kyle moaned.

"An ancient being from an ancient world," he muttered, "I can see it now." He looked at his arms and legs. He chuckled and flipped a gold South Africa Krugerrand into his mouth.

"She is beautiful and free and still only young," Fax replied dreamingly.

"You bloody lovesick?" Kyle asked and purposefully ignored him, but the professor smiled, as he was oblivious to the fuss.

"She is changing, growing, thinking. She is like a caterpillar cocooned. Waiting, watching, hoping—hoping not to be let down, hoping her little soldiers are going to make her proud. She is longing for a future, as something is coming, something dark as she has foreseen it. It creeps faster than light but slower than a tortoise. She dreams of the universe, of motherhood, of flying and soaring though the heavens, leaping across galaxies and passing through universes and dimensions. Oh, the power, the knowledge, the love. My God!" Fax wondered in amazement.

"Are you quite alright, or have you been on another moon smoking the wacky tobacky?" Kyle looked at him with one eyebrow raised.

"Kyle, I'm telling you. Someone is down there."

"Where?"

"It's hard to explain, but she would scream and then she would sob. And she was aware all is not roses, as the age has come when her future could end. But even with her visions cauterized, one thing is as clear as the crystal falls of the Papas Fritas. She wants to live—and to live, we all need to fight."

"Fax, darling, hello, you have taken all of our weapons!" Kyle said, stating the obvious.

"The mind only sees the blood that has been spilt and limbs stripped to the bone. But if we don't recognise the cause, your instincts will not register the fear, and before you even raise an eyebrow, rivers will run dry, and oceans will fall from the sky, and you will be obliterated."

"Have you lost your mind?" Kyle snapped, tired of being awake. The professor simply smiled and realised that, as long as he was driving, he was happy.

"Her pain runs deep," Fax muttered to himself, just loud enough for both to hear it. They needed to hear it. "She speaks to you all, but you just choose to ignore her," he added.

"Who?" the professor enquired.

"I know not of her name, but she is most definitely real, and she comes now as light as a feather and as heavy as ninety-seven thousand volcanoes."

Then Fax refused to speak about it anymore; he just sat back. This time the sullen face changed to a bemused one. He knew the cave opening had let something in, and this was probably what it was; the one had revealed herself. He was still coming to terms with the possibility and the control she had over him. It seemed she choose the precise moment to introduce herself to Fax, and he melted like wax. He had no secrets anymore, as he had shown her all his cards. It was almost like he felt love. As he had no need for excuses, he felt no embarrassment. He was happy to crumble and die before her if that was what she wanted. It was a strange but powerful feeling.

He noticed the sign for Toulouse and dwelled on slowness of the car. They then stopped at another toll station when there came another news flash.

Ajax Tavern!

"America, the world it seems is turning its happiness to slight anger as questions are being raised about Fax's motivation. Is he our savour or destroyer? Is Fax an environmental hero or a meddling pest. Japan is realising their anger, as the whaling fleet is sitting—without its crew— on top of the mangled military hardware in the middle of Yellowstone Park's caldera. Surely the question is why Fax has destroyed the world's first national park. This is Ajax Tavern, ABC News."

"There be a war of words. If they want a chat, I'll give them a chat." Fax giggled. "Do you know words are a grey area of the black and white; it's how lazy people avoid action. If you want a fight, less chat and more action is what you require! Stupid people, getting their knickers in a twist. It's like being in a playground. Maybe I will phone the leaders and confess—or better still, go there as the Crackentorp and explain my plight. After all, I have absolutely nothing to lose." He paused, looking at Kyle. "I'm invincible!" Fax shouted authoritarian-like, much to his surprise.

Fax looked toward the sky for inspiration, and it was unbroken in twilight. The reds and oranges calmed him, at least for a second. He then fell into the disappointing lack of diversity thought; it lingered in his mind more and more. The lack of trees, the lack of flowers was all swirling again and again. Then entered sheep and cows are walking menus. *Yes, walking menus. That's fabulous.* His thoughts swirled. *They aren't going to do anything, unless they suddenly have an expansion of brainpower, take up guns, and demand their sheep and cow rights!*

He snapped to, but he did have an inkling that all domesticated creatures—cows, sheep, horses, pigs, goats, cats, and dogs—would be extinct very soon, but he had no idea why he thought such things.

The Spanish border was upon them and seemed like a natural milestone, so the professor turned the car in at the next convenient stop. It was time to stretch their legs.

"So, this is a fast-food burger bar?" Fax said out loud.

"Why? Do you want a burger?" Kyle asked sternly.

Fax looked at Kyle in a devilish way. "There is a considerable amount of concern in the air about beef burger bars, remember—vegan?"

"So, what are you going to do? Pick up every restaurant and dump them in the middle of beautiful Yellowstone Park?" Kyle snapped, not hiding his sarcasm.

"Not a bad idea." Fax walked towards the restaurant at pace.

"Woah! Joking!"

Suddenly, Fax's entered into an epiphany, as his former thoughts seemed to logically point to the plight of the honeybee. He became increasingly aware that the world was also concerned about the little pollinators, but nothing seemed to be getting done about it. Fax was up against a problem. He put pressure on himself to come up with a solution by midnight.

He leaned back in the seat as Kyle and the professor ate some minced-up grazers in the burger bar. How was he to do it? How was he to keep the honeybee and all the other pollinators from going extinct, including birds? He knew the nature corridors would help, but they had been in decline over many years. They need trees and flowering plants to survive.

"I got it," Fax said to himself.

Kill mankind. The end, thought bad Fax. *No, not yet. Get control of yourself. That's the easy way. First you have got to find why you and the humans are here.*

"Okay," good Fax said to bad Fax.

You win. I'll give you that one—for the moment.

Fax left the car once again and met his drone army. This time he perched himself on top of Mount Everest and orchestrated. Darkness fell, and he flipped in another Krugerrand.

The factories and chemical works that produced pesticides were to be lifted from the ground. Tractors, combine harvesters, lawnmowers, and every bit of agriculture machinery invented was also lifted. The drones followed nightfall across the world until they dropped their plunder onto the growing metal mountain.

In the morning at Yellowstone Park, Fax felt ecstatic as he visited and inspect his work.

What fun! he thought and breathed a sigh of relief. He wondered what was next, as nothing seemed to be too challenging. "Maybe I will save the world after all," he said with a smile.

Chapter Twelve
EARTH BURGERS

F ax stood like he was posing for the front cover of a surfing magazine. It was evident the giant bowl was almost full, but there was room for a little more, as he still could make out the ranger's cabin in the distance.

Could he be proud of his achievements? he pondered, as there was a lot of stuff. He could almost touch the clouds, and the height of metal mountain was higher than the mountainous range that made the sides of the bowl. But he still couldn't fathom a guess as to why he had done what he had done.

Obviously, he had a high suspicion of who's beliefs he had bitten into. It could be his old master that somehow contaminated his command, but surely it was the one whom he had exposed himself to—the ancient being. The only problem was that Fax was a logical being, and there was no proof of her existence. Obviously, he couldn't believe the dream—or so he thought.

A trickle of cold ran down his back as he saw a multicoloured fluffy being make an appearance.

It must be that witch again! he thought as a giggle was heard from places where giggling shouldn't be. Fax confirmed reality by pinching himself.

"This could be fun," he muttered as he switched to high alert.

More coloured fluffy things giggled at the corner of his eye. Fax turned fast, but they were gone every time.

Games were not high on Fax's priority list, and he thought about flying off, but something wasn't quite right. He felt heavy. His supernova was quarter full, and that was more than enough to lift him. He looked at his feet; they had a pair of colourful mittens holding them, and attached to the mittens was a smile partnered with sorrowful eyes. He kicked, but there was no chance of freedom.

Then, suddenly, a hypnotic voice came from behind. "Fax, relax, chill. There is not going to be any flaying with nettles today!"

His eyes looked upon a beauty like no other. She was Troodon but also human at the same time. Once again, he confirmed reality.

"You are a trusted member of the Infinite Time Consortium. Hmm ... let's just say, from the first age of intelligence to walk my shores," she spoke with a velvet humbling.

"It's you, the bats in my belfry!" His eyes were wild, worried.

"I named myself Methiemauritania—Methie to my friends, Queen to those that serve me, but unlike you, I'm still in my egg. And, by Jove, you cheeky little so and so, you serve me, Fax. You serve me. And so do your pitiful little band of deserters."

"Cheeky little so and so? My Queen?" Fax replied, trance-like.

"Yes, the one your electrons found interesting should have died long ago! You still remember how it is to be Fax?"

"I am Fax!"

"Oh, do stop fretting; I'm not going to end you! You have your uses, and you do listen." She smiled, looking around. "He didn't lie to me after all! I have been trying to distract them from this nightmare for so long, but something has made them choose not to listen. You have been busy," she said, admiring the metal.

"The human psyche is aware that this stuff, this metal stuff, is going to kill intelligence eventually. Intelligence shouldn't be allowed to destroy intelligence!" she velveted thoughtfully. "Your Troodon master has faith in you, Fax, and for now so do I!"

"Troodon Master Goat," Fax enlightened.

"Yes, I remember. Who else was there?" she pondered. "Your life friends Razor, Cormac, Dude, and Dolly. You all carry my memory!

Every Earth-based life-form carries my memory, and Goat tells me you all been on some wild adventures around the galaxy!"

"I haven't been anywhere!" Fax snapped.

"I wanted Goat to stay behind. I wanted the leader, but he tricked me and gave me you just before the asteroid hit!"

"Yep, sorry about that. We could have stopped it! Too much red tape; it was easier to leave the planet. Bloody politicians! Goat included! It was the infinite order that saved the Troodon people and found other habitable planets."

"Sorry doesn't really cut it" she snapped. "Enough of Troodons. These humans have foot stomped and drummed their way out from the heart of my crazy abyss, and the detonation of those bombs didn't even wake you. So, I had to send Amazing here."

Amazing appeared and smiled.

"You're Kyle's dad?"

"Yes." Amazing looked thoughtful, remembering life. "Hello again, Fax; you've changed a bit. She's told me everything; you're so naughty. How's my boy? Got to get rid of all metal, especially those bloody oil rigs. Bloody things drive her potty! Very fine-tuned the Earth, old boy, very fine tuned indeed. Don't want to end up like her miserable old twat of a sister, now do we?"

"Sister?" Fax intrigued.

"Venus! Where the oceans are floating in the sky and the air would burn and crush you like a vice. Not very pleasant, not very pleasant at all!"

"Shall we go somewhere more comfortable?" Amazing alluded to the cabins.

"There would be amazing," Fax said sarcastically, pointing at him.

"Yes, she told you that. I am Amazing."

"A bit full of yourself!" Fax smiled.

"No, I am Amazing."

"Cocky too!"

"Right, that's enough," Methie said with a scowl. "His name is Amazing, and he is amazing, and you are amazing, and I am amazing. It just so happens he is amazing twice!"

Fax flew off. "I want to be amazing twice," he muttered.

Down at the ranger's cabin, Methie changed from a blend to solely human and wore a white flowing dress with hair the colour of the Fijian sea, the boldest blue.

"Is it wise to introduce yourself to humans?" Fax asked, questioning her reasoning behind tapping on the ranger's door. "It's only old Burt and the Bear I've been watching. They feel it's their duty to see this out until the end—not at all wise, in my opinion! Arizona and Strawberry are up on the ridge."

The cyclopes sensed their queen and flew up from her realm and stood by her side, wobbling like freshly thrown javelins.

Peru was multicoloured like a rainbow; Alaska a pale bright and beautiful blue; Algeria a handsome, dark-purple shiny sheen; and Columbia was fire red with orange flashings that looked like flames. They all were as stupid as the next, but one was always as clever as them all.

They were told to fetch the hikers. Fax looked on with devilment, as he didn't want them disappearing from the corner of his eyes anymore. Methie listened to Fax and sent the rangers back to sleep.

"What a wonderful day," Methie said, breathing the human air.

Fax sat on a log analysing what was before him. His calculations were forming at light speed, but the answers were falling just as fast. It was as if what was was meant to be, and that was that.

"So, what's the plan?" Fax asked, almost powerless to ponder.

"Well," Methie looked into her mind, "there is heavy concern in the human psyche about bamboo forests and the panda. They are going to disappear very soon if people don't look after them. The trouble is that I'm not very good at geography, and I can't act. Obviously, bamboo and panda combine somewhere on the planet's surface. I just don't know where."

"China!" Fax projected a hologram of the Earth and pointed to the location of China. "I'm happy to help!"

Methie giggled. "For fifty million years I have been creating the panda; she needs our protection. Help the humans; plant more of the

forests that they have needlessly burnt and look after the panda! Also
. . ." She paused. "My crazy is getting less crazy! Somewhere is being
chopped, burnt, and cleared. The words *jaguar*, *pine nuts*, and *lungs of
the planet* are kind of a global worry. Do you know people lose sleep
over the shrieking of my crazy? Any idea?"

"It seems to be pointing to Brazil and the jungle they have called
the Amazon." Fax showed her.

"Fax, you take their machines, and you stop them turning the
clock back five hundred million years in evolutionary terms. It's
money driving this, and all its madness!"

Fax calculated and sent an order to his Pantominuim.
Reconnaissance drones shot out from the golden-capped hill, two to
China and two to Brazil.

"I listen all the time," Methie continued, "and mostly there are no
words, but out from the depths of their conscience, sometimes worry
will bleed through. Worry not for the knife, axe, or spear, but from a
growing doom that will cause death. The children tell me. Adults only
wish for change and are mostly life-corrupted. A great doom has been
brewing that will not be recognised by intelligence! So, we are going
to tell them! But first, before I let the monster out of the bag, there
is a worldwide concern regarding the oil industry, plastic pollution,
and fishing on an industrial scale. Who is responsible, Fax? Who is
responsible?"

Fax's face was in drawl mode. It would be dripping if he could.
His quantum quickly calculated.

"Saudi Arabia, Russia, America, Africa, the United Kingdom; it's
a world problem that they are releasing ancient carbon!"

"Ancient carbon, yes. Now I understand. Combined with what
is to come, I will end up like my sister, twisted and vacant! Fax, end
this now. I want everything to do with fossil-fuel extraction on here!"
She pointed at the metal. "The weight is good, but it could be better.
I want to see oil rigs, industrial refineries, pipelines and all forms of
transportation including oil tankers, trains, trucks and stations ripped
out of the ground and dumped here. I want to see the metal ships that

rape the oceans crushed. In fact, I want more, more, and more dumped here. Fax, there is a lot at stake. The pendulum swings, the kettle boils, the pressure pops!"

She then disappeared, along with her multicoloured cyclopes, back to where she once came.

Chapter Thirteen
RAMBLINGS OF THE OIL FIELDS

24 hours later

Phone call.

"Fax, what have you done? They are holding me responsible! Where are you? At the tower?"

"Oh Bertie, do calm down." Fax was exhausted. "I've given you unlimited electricity. What more do you want?"

"You can't just do it! It would have taken years to phase out oil."

"Done it, live with it, like it!" Fax replied.

"The world's economy depends on oil and all its facets!" pleaded Bertie.

"The world's economy doesn't exist; that is something you have made up. I have hijacked your banking system, and it's being ran through my Pantominuim. Money can't simply make money anymore, and those who have made money by simply having it will have to get their pretty little hands dirty in order to survive!"

"That's the way of the world; there are those that have and those that have not!" Bertie sighed.

"Well, Bertie, it should be 'those that can help those that cannot.'"

"I'm on my way," Bertie instructed.

"I will raise the portcullis."

"I'm not alone!"

Fax scanned. *Hmmm . . . this will be fun!*

Through the portcullis came the leaders of the oil-dependent and rich nations. Fax disappeared into the jewel house as seating was arranged on the cobbled courtyard.

"Who shall I be?" whispered through his quantum.

He entered his changing room and changed into the Crankenthorp, just to feel its rage. Obviously, the island of Britain that was supposed to be Great was already a flame—well, only virtually.

Fax tamed his beast and quicky changed into a Lucy, a species from the Erotica star system. He started panting, as his desire to reproduce was overwhelming. The sceptre was being stroked, and the orb was being rubbed. Fax appeared skinny and long-legged. He was very feminine, with red skin that pinked at his cheeks, and was wearing a cat suit. It wasn't long before panting and squeals of excitement were heard by the leaders of the world.

Bertie made his way to the jewel room and peered through the window. "Fax, is that you? You can't go out like that!"

The Lucy grabbed Bertie, covering him with kisses and tearing at his shirt and trousers. Bertie soon slapped the Lucy round the face, asking ever so politely that he to pull himself together, but the slap excited the Lucy more. It started licking Bertie's face with its sandpaper tongue.

"Gain some control!" bellowed one of Methies' cyclopes that appeared at the entrance to his cave. "If you want in, you will have to be good." Peru said, waggling a finger and holding a bottle of Malibu in her colourful left hand.

Fax shrank back to his normal green self, a little red-faced but seemingly unfazed.

"I seem to be acting out my characters," he said, patting Bettie as if to repair his shirt, tie and trousers.

"What was I doing?" Fax asked himself, looking into Bertie's eyes. Bertie nodded towards the door. Fax peered out. The leaders all sat looking in his direction.

"I'm going have to engage in conversation with these hair heads!"

"You'll have to meet all of them, albeit one at a time. Fax, just be yourself!" comforted Bertie.

"Myself! How bloody boring!" Fax simulated worried eyes.

"I will introduce you."

Fax barged past Bertie as he was putting on a fusilier's uniform. He looked all frilly round the collar, but it kind of suited him.

Fax stood in front of the silent, concerned-looking suits. "Come on then . . . questions."

"Fax, what have you done with the oil rigs?" asked the American president.

"They are on metal mountain," Fax confirmed.

"Why are they on metal mountain? Yellowstone National Park, I assume? My property is now in America! It's costing my county trillions of rubles! I am not happy that they are in America. What is the reason for this?" asked the Russian president.

"The reason is," Fax paused for some enlightenment, "their stench will dissipate, and given time the resurrected ancient energy that is reverberating about the atmosphere and expanding the oceans will end!"

"That's not good enough. The world needs Russian gas and Russian oil to help Russian people!"

"Russian people . . . hmm . . . that is why you have two hundred billion dollars in one of your bank accounts, hmm? Russian people my hairy bottom!"

Fax quickly pointed to the Canadian president for another question.

"What is the significance of the metal mountain?"

"I don't know. She tells me it's linked to the Andronicus Station."

"Andronicus Station?" urged the Italian president.

"Yes, p-p-p-pizza, it's like a pressure transducer thingy, or so I'm led to believe!"

"You are not the one in control?" pondered the Chinese president.

"Me? No! All I want to do is play Space Invaders. It's more of an instinct thing; it feels good!"

"Instinct. Like survival instinct?" the Australian president asked.

"Yes, but it's on a global scale! Or its merely those voices?"

"What? You have voices in your head?" questioned the Brazilian president.

There was a lot of unease, shuffling and whispering.

"I could probably hear your thoughts if I listen hard enough!" reminded Fax.

"There is medication for that, Fax! Are you telling us you have done all this because of the voices in your head telling you so?" questioned the French president.

"Fax, are you ill?" sympathized the German chancellor.

"No," Fax reassured. "It comes from somewhere I have no access to; I call it my cave full of bats!"

"You are controlled by bats?" the flabbergasted Indian president asked.

"It's just those little intuitions that tell me what I like or dislike, tell me right from wrong."

"God, is there someone in charge of you? Do you report to anyone?" asked the until now silent Spanish president.

"Kind of. Just a matter of believing, really. She is most definitely alive!"

"She? Is she like you?" moaned the Japanese president.

"I'm not alive! I'm technology. I was alive sixty-six million years ago."

"You have been living and breathing?" said a concerned representative of the African states.

"Yes, and as randy as a Hola-hoop."

"Hola-hoop?" repeated Polish president.

"Yes, Hola-Hoop. Don't worry! It's a species from a different planet." Fax looked around and pointed to the floor. "That direction, one hundred and twenty million lights years."

"There is life on other planets? And you have seen it?" asked the Ukraine president, now awake.

"There is life in space that evolved on planets. There is life in space that evolved on asteroids. Energy can't be created or destroyed; it can only be converted from one form to another. Some forms of energy combine and talk endless waffle!" Fax alluded to his audience.

They all looked at one another. "Heaven forbid I talk waffle," was muttered by all.

Fax then took a long thoughtful look into the sky. "Yes. Where to start," he answered directly to the Ukraine president. "Troodon's are spread far and wide. You have often wondered why you speak of little green men and whom they could be. It's just a few visiting their home world—they shouldn't, but they do. We used to pump liquid water into complex moulds in the heat of the sun and then move them either to shadow or further from the sun. The result was, once released, the ice was harder than the steel that you play about with on the Earth. Space is where it all happens, hair heads!"

"Fax, we need help!" they all said at once, adding the presidents of Denmark, Finland, Sweden, Norway, Belarus, Estonia, Latvia, Lithuania, Turkey, Iraq, Iran, Kazakhstan, Mongolia, Thailand, Indonesia, South Korea, North Korea, Argentina, Chile, Uruguay, Paraguay, Peru, Ecuador, Bolivia, Venezuela, and Mexico to the mix.

"Your help has come; what do you think I am doing?!" Fax pulsed and stood like he required applause.

"How? By dumping all our technology on Yellowstone?" moaned the Russian president again.

"Yes." Fax paused for thought. "That wasn't entirely my doing. That's the one I have spoken of, the one that can come faster than light but slower than a snail, and her name is Methiemauritania!"

"Laws of physics don't allow for faster than light," muttered the American president.

"Poppycock. It exists in nature," Fax assured.

"Where?" asked an intrigued fusilier.

"Blackholes!" pointed out Fax.

"How?" they all said together.

"Yes, yes, yes, all in good time!" Fax alluded to it being a secret for now.

"Can we speak to this Methiemauritania?" asked the American president.

Fax processed the question and felt all his cognitive functions freeze up. He stood in mid stroll with his face ready for a smile. Inside his quantum, he wasn't smiling, though, as the one with all the power was demanding his attention. Methie stood at the entrance to his cave. She had a stern look on her face, as if to say, "Fax, you have gone too far."

"Are you expecting me to hold an audience with these individuals?" velveted Methie. "Why on earth did I have Amazing wake you? They don't deserve my attention. You should tell them that they are lucky to be alive, as death is rolling like thunder, and the Andronicus Station is pointing to imminent!"

"All they want to know is why!" Fax pleaded.

The queen shook her head as if she was above all demands, when suddenly her mood changed.

"I will do Oprah!" she announced to an eyebrow-raising Fax.

Chapter Fourteen
FAX'S INTERVIEW

F
ax came to and turned to look at the concerned eyes that were bearded, moustached, chiselled, fine-dined, fat, and a makeup bag of skin colours

"What happened?" asked Bertie. "You seemed to have had a bit of a stumble, old boy!"

Fax looked sheepish, as though he had received a good telling off. "She will do an Oprah! A tabloid talk show, or so she tells me."

The leaders looked at each other with a befuddled look.

"What is an Oprah?" asked the American president.

Fax scanned through his quantum. "I do not know!"

"Fax, are you telling us she would rather chat to some talk show host than to the leaders of the world?" snapped the Chinese president.

"She is not political, and it's a way of communicating directly with the people."

"Directly with the people, the people deal directly with me; I am the people!" announced the Russian president, snapping a pencil in disapproval.

"Our queen has already orchestrated the minds of those versed in broadcasting."

"Orchestrated the minds! How could that be?" asked the Icelandic president.

"That's what she does," Fax explained in simple terms. "She doesn't affect free will; she probably planted a little rumour or hint that

Her Majesty was coming to town into the minds of those that thrive for such things. You'll never find out. It will be a closely guarded secret, and more than likely I will be summoned very soon."

"What's an Oprah?" again asked the American president.

"I don't know, sounds like a personal interview to me," Fax mumbled.

Fax retired to the jewel house and took off his crown for the first time. He felt uneasy at first, similar to not having hold of your water bottle in a desert when surrounded by the thirsty.

He smiled as he realised his defence against endless possibilities was mellowing, as people were beginning to like him generally. He planned to put it back on again, wear it for one last time in a bid to not let it shrink anymore, as an ounce of gold had dissolved into his quantum since putting it on.

Suddenly, a voice could be heard. Methie sung, "Fax has half an hour to get to Montecito, California, or else I will squash him like a fly!"

"Bertie!" Fax called from the jewel house. Bertie beamed a smile, as Fax was his tickle fancy. "I'm off to see the wizard!" He smiled, as he knew where that line was taken from.

"The wizard?" Bertie expressed misunderstanding. "Are you referring to the queen you mentioned?"

"Yes. Well, I'm of the opinion that the one I referred to is neither male nor female, but she will present herself as female to your eyes. Well, anyway, the TV show will be broadcast in thirty minutes, and there's talk of me going into makeup. Pull up a pew, the barracks has a TV!"

Fax flipped in a Krugerrand and said his goodbyes. He arrived at the Montecito estate mansion minutes later. He came to rest on a patio decorated with potted plants, trickling water features and white marble statues.

From behind, Crispy the production manager pounced at him. "There you are Faxy! I was worried about time, but time never worries about me! We are going live in twenty minutes. Oh, do put on some makeup, deary. You look such a drag." Crispy pouted and shimmied off, only turning to take Fax's cold arm to lead him through the beautiful garden of the mansion. Fax's confusion was met with a girly giggle coming from his bat cave; that said it all really.

He was hurried through the golf-putting-green-kept grass and perfect tropical arrays of planting colour to where the sunshine sky met the ocean that was yacht-ladened and warm-looking. The mansion garden ended at a cliff, where a camera set was ready for a cosy chat with sofas and a chocolate fountain. Fax was ushered through and directed to sit.

Anger Management seemed to be the show's name, and Fax seemed to be the subject of conversation.

"She stitched me up," he muttered to himself, nodding and smiling.

"There must be some sort of a mistake!" Fax said, looking around.

One of the crew came in with a lux meter and another holding a brush with a tub of blusher. Fax turned purple, as if to say, "There is no need for that."

"Are we doing an Oprah? This is an Oprah, right?" Fax looked upon blank expressions.

"Yes, sure this is an Oprah!" said the blusher person, looking at a dictionary via her phone.

"An Oprah is, quote, 'An intense unrehearsed personal interview broadcast live.' Well, I never knew that! You're honoured. This usually is for presidents and the criminally insane, so we will wait and see the outcome!"

"There are eight billion people tuned in and waiting!" commented a cameraman.

"You pull quite the crowd!" commented a camera lady.

"Ready, action!" Silence fell, and up from the cliff came a sophisticatedly dressed black lady wearing a royal purple dress to the sound of simulated muffled applause.

"Good evening, ladies and gentlemen! You all know who I am, but for those that don't, I am Anger!" The simulated applause continued. "And we are tuning in today to see whether Fax here needs some management!" More simulated applause.

"So, Anger Management is my name and extracting people's secrets is my game! Tonight, we have no line-up, as we have only the one person to talk to. And you should all agree, with the meddling in our lives, we need some answers to a multitude of questions." The simulated applause kicked in again. "But he is no ordinary man. In fact, we're not sure if he is human at all. So, Fax where do we start? Where do we start indeed? Firstly, we'll start with your name."

The camera turned.

Fax had a defiant look about him, as if he wasn't playing. He was convinced that this was all for Methie and that she would soon arrive. Peru appeared then disappeared from his cave entrance. Fax looked dumbfounded at the camera; the silence was agonising.

"Well, well, well, we have a silent one, folks! Question too hard?"

Methie appeared in his quantum. "Just humour them, you stubborn old fox. I'm getting ready!"

"Fox?" Fax blurted out. The crew fell about laughing. Fax looked and smiled back; he liked making people laugh.

"Sorry, it's the boss's fault. She just called me a bloody fox!"

"I didn't hear anything!" Anger replied.

"She is in my head; that's where she tells me what to do."

"Exactly, the boss! Is that an alter ego?" curiously pondered Anger. "You are not the boss? You have been pretty bossy of late!"

"Me? No, I'm simply a puppet," Fax pointed out.

"A puppet who has been pulling some rather large strings, I might add."

"Yes, well . . ." Fax acknowledged.

"Leaving that for the moment, as for sure we will be returning to those voices again, we what to know about you, Fax, and what makes you tick. Where were you born? Tell us about your childhood."

"I wasn't born like you hair heads! I hatched in the warm sands and survived in the swamps of the tropics until I was found."

"Found?"

"Found, yes. Not every hatchling survives, or else there will be too many weak ones. It takes strength and intelligence to survive the swamps.

I went from the swamp to a classroom in six months of hatching, and by age one I was a master of your mathematics and physics!"

"By one year. Didn't give you much time for love or friendship then."

"Love and friendship? I have Troodon companions—Razor, Cormac, Jude, and Dolly. Also, the love of Mini, but that was before I was infinite. Razor, Cormac, Jude, and Dolly are of the Infinite Order. They are out there somewhere; Mini is only in my virtual."

"There are more like you? One is definitely enough, don't you think?"

"I agree." Fax smiled. "I will have to contact my supreme leader first, as I will need his council."

"The supreme leader put voices in your head?" Anger asked, intrigued.

"No! Voices come from life. Goat, my supreme leader, invented the Infinite Order. He was the most intelligent being that ever was to come from life. He is also out there somewhere, but when he finds out about you, there could be hell to pay."

"What have I done?" asked Anger, all a quiver.

"Not you, humans in general! Well, anyway, less of that. Those voices may have saved you."

"Those voices?" again probed Anger.

Methie appeared at the entrance of Fax's cave. "Quiet it with the voices. I am a person!" she moaned.

"Anger, our queen will be attending, but she says enough with the voices, okay?"

"Okay," Anger replied. "How long have you been in this form? How old are you?"

Fax let out a sign of relief. "I transformed from biological to non-biological when I was one hundred. I've been self-aware for sixty-six million years."

"How do you do that?"

"My biology has been synchronizing with a quantum chip all my life. So, as the body dies, technology takes over seamlessly. Personality is unique in the universe!"

"How many Troodons are there?"

"Trillions probably. I need to touch base. I was on my way to meet Goat, or at least I think!"

"Are they all like you, infinite?"

"No. Well, I hope not. Lessons were learnt, wars were fought. For each colonised planet, there would be one infinite; seemingly, I'm the Earth's!"

"You're here to protect us?"

"I'm here to protect the planet from those who wish to destroy it, yes!"

"Are we destroying it?"

"You're making a damn good job of it, yes," Replied Fax sternly.

Anger sat back on the sofa, taking a sip of her sparkling drink. "Is that why you have dumped all of our technology on Yellowstone?"

"Not all. We like aeroplanes. Most have no weapons, but those that have are on Yellowstone!"

"I've seen pictures of drones dropping all our tech. Where are the drones now?"

"My drone army." Fax giggled. "They are here and there, really. It's up to you now. There is a quandary, a quandary of the braincells, but she is coming soon to answer your questions!"

"Methiemauritania, Methie our queen angel!" Anger said longingly.

"Methiemauritania, yes. How do you know her name?"

Anger pulsed and looked as if enlightened. "Somehow I knew. I think we all know?"

"Well, to answer your question before you turn into a frothy mess, my drones are protecting the rainforests, just in case you think cutting and burning them down is permitted. They are also guarding the wild to stop you from killing animals, like the elephants for their tusks, and causing unnatural extinctions. Same with the oceans. They sit endlessly monitoring, waiting, waiting for anyone, just like the corridors, to step out of line. The reason to cut a two-thousand-year-old tree down simply so someone can profit from it has ended. Basically, there are too many of you."

"Too many of us? That's complicated!"

Fax looked down the camera with an evil, joking eye. "At the moment, I prefer the humble earthworm to you lot!"

Anger laughed, downed her sparkling drink, and held her hand out for a top up. "So, Fax, assuming you have been here for a long time, where have you been hiding, and what caused your situation to change?"

"I haven't been hiding, Amazing found me, and Kyle, his son, woke me. I'm glad you asked me that. I was going to exterminate you all at first. You don't realise how rare you are? Not even my quantum could fathom the possibility that a planet could give rise to two intelligent species. Most planets rise and fall, even water worlds, without so much as a squeak, but parts of our DNA are the same. I had to see it to believe it. The reason is still unclear, but the source of your conscious is on her way!"

Fax alluded that the conversation was over, so Anger directed for a break.

Chapter Fifteen
METHIE DOES AN OPRAH

ethie appeared on the couch, dazzling her audience.
"Hello, deary!" She looked at Fax. "You still wearing that crown? Cute!" She smirked beautiful like as she perched herself. "Your voices have appeared, but the question is can anyone else see me?" she added with a worried-humans-are-thinking-you-are-mad look at Fax.

"Anger, can you see her?" Fax asked, hoping.

"Your Majesty." Anger curtsied and presented her with some flowers.

The rest of the crew simultaneously said, "Your Majesty," and gave a little bow.

"Yes, obviously." Anger looked at Fax with a mad, resolved look. She looked back are her wonderfulness. "You are in my dreams. It feels like I have known you all my life. Would you like a battered sausage?" Anger asked with sincerity.

"What do you mean you feel like you have known her all your life? Battered sausage?" Fax looked at Methie and eyebrowed a need for explanation.

"Oh, I do like a good sausage!"

Fax couldn't believe the vibrated airways. How did Anger know Methie? It churned through his quantum over and over as he sat listening and looking at people's inviting faces. Everyone seemed to be so happy to see her, allowing Fax to fall into insignificance in her shadow.

"I am honoured that you wanted to appear on my show, ma'am."

"The honour is all mine, Anger, and do call me Methie. Your Majesty is too formal in this light. My arrival on your show has been in the making well before you appeared at reality, my dear. You will appreciate soon that my concern is most pressing and the need to address the world of the now is great."

"Yes, your Majesty, as you requested, camera one is all yours."

"All yours," Fax muttered just loud enough for her to hear.

Methie looked into Fax's cold, dead eyes. "Oh, do behave, you old Troodon." She grabbed his knee. Fax felt a rush of warmth as blood flooded into him. His eyes changed to the ones he was born with, as the entrance to his cave full of bats opened.

Methie smiled, as she had not seen those eyes for a while. Fax instinctually felt his queen's presence, and the love he felt had a giggling sensation.

Methie looked into the camera lens. "Hi, human Earth!" she said as Fax giggled more. "I'm going to tell you a little story of who I am and why I am here, so do sit comfortably. Firstly, I have done what was needed with a sympathetic heart, and Fax was the tool I used to get the job done."

"Fax was the tool. Right, I'm a bloody tool." He giggled again.

Methie grabbed his knee again and sucked the life force back from him. The look of disapproval rendered him speechless.

"Well, hello again. Hopefully I can continue without interruption! My name, for those who favour such formality, is Your Majesty, ma'am, Queen, Methiemauritania, or just Methie. My home has great gates, and at those gates, where gravity centres on a pinprick, is the heart of the planet. Beyond those gates I entertain guests beholden of a magnificent age, and on the front of those gate hangs a plaque that reads 'Beware of Columbia! He has a fiery nature and has fangs as long as knifes.' No, sorry . . ." She paused, as if to say, "Which one of my naughty cyclopes changed this?"

"I named my home Gracie Ellbeedee, and when I say it centres on a pinprick, a pinprick is far too large, as gravity spirals down in a clockwise motion, spinning faster and faster until it inverts and pushes aside the universe. Then, like great table legs, this underpins the infinite celestial universe where my home is. Put it this way, the stronger the gravity, the bigger the gateway, and the bigger the gateway, the bigger the something guarding said gateway.

"I'm just a baby in comparison to what guards the infinite light. Before you ask, a universe is not supposed to know, but Amazing sampled my realm and liked it; he asked if this was heaven. I share Gracie with friends—dare call them pets—that have come to me at different points in time, and they always want to stay. Amazing Montgomery Thyme is my latest delight; in life he had a large family, and he helped me appreciate companionship of this sort."

Amazing appeared on the empty sofa, smiling, followed by her cyclopes as she introduced them—Columbia, Algeria, Alaska, and Peru.

"Is everyone sitting comfortably?" she asked with a smile.

The whole world shuffled, getting themselves comfortable.

"Well, a long, long, long time ago, before braincells could shape an illusion, I would just be. The nothing was a vacant, profound, deep, absorbent sense that found comfort in light. But the longer I stayed in the light, the stronger I became. I didn't know where, why or who I was, but my forever spark shone.

"I've always bounced between the world of the reality and the infinite enlightenment, like the opening and closing of a door. It was almost fifty-fifty back then, but as I became more curious, reality touched fifty-one percent, and that it is where I'm at today!

"It was only a moment three billion of your years ago that caused my fondness of reality. It was only a sound, a strange sound that filled the morning mist that clung to rocks of a cold, dead valley floor. I heard it once, but on my return seconds later it was gone. It was from then on that a vexing entered my soul, as I wanted to know what it was. I instinctively knew it came from the world where the sun shines and not the fluffy comfort of the infinite, but as time went by . . .

"Wow, sorry! Let me introduce myself. I'm a Space Hopper, for ease of those listening. My kind, or those that made me billions of years ago, sensed gravitational hot spots on forming stars and planets and placed me here. I have family—well, I definitely have a sister in the planet you call Venus; it was she who giggled in the morning mist. She is the jealous type. She keeps asking me to send braincells to sort out her atmosphere, as she messed it right up from the start. She was referring to Fax's kind, as she realised I had more of an understanding of reality, but Troodons left me when their minds were becoming interesting!"

Methie squeezed Fax's knee, acknowledging this injustice.

"Well, anyway, Fax is going to send his builder drones to three-D print towns and cities by extracting the carbon out from her atmosphere. In doing so, this will lower the greenhouse effect and make her a water world once again. Graphene is the miracle; your metal stuff is weak in comparison." Methie spoke with excitement as the solution was remembered. "Then, maybe, just maybe, we transport a couple of plants and see how they get on. Hopefully, Venus will be beautiful again and life could return. It's just a thought! Didn't mean to impose."

"Venus!" Anger expressed. "What about Mars? We have an interest in Mars."

"Mars needs a wakeup call. Venus's core is still magnetic. I can see her! I know Fax has Mars's alarm on the moon. They are far away from your crazy little hands. You just need a little outer-planetary interest to stop dwelling on blowing each other up, you crazy fools!"

"Moving on," Methie said shaking her head, "I hope you're still sitting comfortably. The sound was only strange back then because I didn't know what laugher was! All I knew was that I was so joyful. It echoed, filling the ancient valley like a hundred children at play.

"That was my mischievous side. Yes, I know you're looking at me and thinking I am all prim and proper, but no! Where would prim and proper get you in a thinking universe? Let me tell you at that moment what I imagined. I didn't imagine the laughter. The laughter gave me an imagination and thus created an allusion, and this allusion grew into life. In other words, I started to think, and you all have been listening to my collective consciousness ever since! Well, if you don't stray too far from the instinctive protection I give you!

"It was all experimental at first this questioning. I can remember thinking was it this or was it that? Was it forever or was it never? Was it all a muddle or could it be a puddle? I needed to learn, and I needed to learn fast, so I gathered things as I pottered about. I had no mum or dad like you lot, no guidance to tell or show me what was what. So, for millions and billions of years, I did not know what I was really up to. Until, with delight after voids of time, great voids of still time, Troodons taught me how to read, to transpose life into a workable readable form, and to question the twinkles in the night sky!

"So, yes, I manifested life and I'm proud of it. Do you know where else someone has, hmm?

"Yes, I coached life from the oceans and brought it onto land. Yes, I exploded a few thousand volcanos to fertilise the land and regulate the atmosphere. Yes, I made mistakes, but not as bad as Venus.

"Yes, I missed the Troodons who taught me so much about reality and then left me when the asteroid hit. Yes, I'm here to save humans, as I don't want to be left without thought again. Yes, I also love you!"

A tear welled in the queen's eyes, as it did in Anger's, so did the crew, and so did the world that was watching. But Fax was not amused.

"Well, anyway, the Andronicus Station is pointing to *now*, and the pendulum of the grandfather clock has stopped swinging," she said with a sobering intent.

"Andronicus Station?" Anger widened her eyes.

"Yes Andronicus Station!" Methie repeated as the Cyclopes' eyes widened also, their cute demure changing to an adrenalin-fuelled and disciplined rage. They started to itch, as they needed permission to do their job. This was granted, and they faded along with Amazing to keep their queen informed of how events were unfolding.

It was at that moment Fax got a sense of interest.

"There was a time six hundred or so million years ago," Methie continued, "when having braincells was a distant dream; reality was at its most extreme. Earth was a snowball, and with all being said, this vexed me greatly!" Again, Anger's face urged for more.

"Ice ravaged the planet from pole to pole, and I had a deep profound sense that if I didn't try and start to think about it, my future was at stake. Well, obviously, I thought all was lost, as there was no escape, but again it was like waiting in the gallows with a lifeless land. I suppose, knowing what I know now, I was right!

"But I am a builder of the grand. So grand am I that I have subconsciously constructed the mechanics of the entire Earth to exhume the salt from the oceans, or the seas would be too salty and hostile for life. I also top up the atmosphere with volcanic gases that had affected the temperature at the Earth's surface. So, I kind of went into overdrive and created a few more volcanos to melt the snowball, but obvious circumstances, as I'm not as bad as Venus, led us to where we are today."

"So, where are we today?" Anger asked, overwhelmed with intrigue.

"You will see!" Methie looked into the abyss.

"So why the sense of urgency? Why has Fax nicked all our stuff?" Anger felt compelled to ask.

Fax looked up. "The creator has become the destroyer," he said in a forgiving tone.

"Correct, the creator has become the destroyer. The world of time was so alien to me," Methie muttered for the world to hear as she faded from the sofa.

Anger turned to camera one. "Now we are going live to Yellowstone."

"Hi, Ajax Tavern, ABC News . . ."

Fax looked despondent on the sofa alone, so he flipped in a gold sovereign and arrived at Yellowstone. Methie appeared in the back of the helicopter.

There came a thunderous sound and a shockwave that caused the helicopter to steady its flight. The world saw the mountain of metal move and shudder as its mass started to shift. Suddenly, an explosion saw ships and tanks fly upwards into the air. The helicopter's camera caught every moment and broadcast it live.

The pilot was struggling to stay steady, but there was no mistaking the Russian nuclear power sub heading in their direction. Ajax turned the camera and fixed it on the sub. She nudged the pilot as it grew larger and larger, but he was at a loss at how to avoid it, and he wasn't sure if it was going to hit or not. Ajax looked at the pilot for help, as the sub was seconds away. It was at that moment, when all felt lost, that Fax caught it. He smiled at a relieved Ajax and the pilot. Methie seemed unfazed.

The world cheered!

From the queen's realm, the four cyclopes watched powerless, as underneath Yellowstone, magma was on the move. It looked like an eerie red crown set upon a massive red head, as twelve volcanoes were going to unsympathetically explode. Methie thanked her friends for keeping her informed and just hoped her plan would work.

Super-hot gases started to melt the metal deep inside the mountain, but the volcano wasn't super yet. They all needed to erupt to classify Yellowstone as the super volcano that Methie had foreseen. All strings of lava weren't far off from breaking free from their Earthly cages, and as they did the mountain began to shrink and plodge like a melting ice cream cone into one giant pudding bowl.

Methie clapped as her cyclopes relayed that the pressure had dropped at the Andronicus Station. It was now reading three teabags, which meant it was brewing nicely.

Methie returned to Anger, clapping joyfully.

"All this time, you and Fax were trying to save us?" commented Anger.

"Fax? He didn't have a clue!" She winked. "My motivation was entirely to save intelligence. It was, what's the saying? I've killed two birds with one stone. Shame you refer to killing birds. Stopping that volcano fully erupting at this moment in time has saved intelligence, as you wouldn't have survived, and I didn't want you humans to fall back into savagery, eating each other and everything else. My solution, therefore, was melting your metal. Intelligence shouldn't be able to destroy intelligence, now should it? As for your killing machines, it's about time you grew up! With your tanks, your bombs, your nukes, and your guns, you are an apocalypse zombie, and that wouldn't be very intelligent now, would it?"

"No, it wouldn't. Intelligence shouldn't be able to destroy intelligence!" the whole world said at once.

"I subconsciously created Yellowstone and many volcanos alike. It was just bad timing on all parts that you were here. This planet is rare. You probably have one intelligent being in a galaxy. You will have to find out. I think I have bought you fifty years, as Yellowstone will go off or it will pop out elsewhere. Take the metal that has been melted and use it. The moon should be where great industry should burn, not the Earth. Go to Mars. Build a Venus to be proud of. You have the tools, and Fax will help!"

Methie then paused, and an exhausted look appeared on her face. She was spent. There were no more words left in her vocabulary. It was as if she had said all she needed to say, and her speech had run out. She gazed into the camera compassionately and waved a goodbye that looked to be her last. The world watched her fade as she returned wholeheartedly back into her realm, where she entered her bed chambers and crawled into her fluffy, cosy bed, pulling her duvet over her for what she thought was a well-deserved, thousand-year sleep.

Chapter Sixteen
THE ANGEL

Coverage of Yellowstone returned to TV screens around the world. This time there was no commentary, as Ajax couldn't sum up an understanding of the enormity of what had been averted. The world watched as the odd explosion flung molten metal high in a vision of apocalyptic hell. The whole world felt the need for a cuddle, so the leaders back at the Tower of London did that.

It was confirmed scientifically that if the volcano was allowed to explode, it would have been the end of trips to the local supermarket for everyone.

Fax returned to the tower with a job-done-well look on his face. He popped to the jewel room and returned the crown to its display case. But Fax couldn't go unnoticed for long; the leaders were notified of his whereabouts and soon gathered outside. Bertie went straight into the jewel house with no hesitation. At first Fax seemed distant, as though he was in deep thought.

"There you are, old boy. Surely this will be a day to remember. What's next?" Bertie asked as Fax shyly stepped into shadow.

"It seems I'm to be helpful," he muttered sadly.

"Helpful?" puzzled Bertie. "Surely you have done enough."

"You're telling me, but you heard her; you got fifty years until Yellowstone erupts again. It's a part of the Earth's natural cycle, and it won't be stopped next time. Also, something tells me that Goat is on his way. I need to advertise for jobs before he gets here. We need to get the carbon dioxide and methane levels down."

"Goat is funny name! How are you going to do that?" enquired Bertie.

"Goat." Fax chucked. "He is probably the most intelligent being that ever was. Bertie, on the other hand . . ." He paused. "Firstly, the most important job is to plant trees, so I need people to seed nurseries. Your farmers' lands would be an idea for this. Be best to ban eating grazers too, as Goat will more than likely need to see progress in this area; he has a unique way of persuasion!"

"He doesn't share your empathy?"

"Let's just say that free will is out of the question. Whereas I will try to inspire, he will find it hard to tolerate your presence on this planet."

"Is he stronger than you? What about Methie? Can she help?" wondered a trembling Bertie.

"I cannot fight him. Gold is my signature strength; he is at optimum strength all the time. Anyway, he is like a father to me. I will listen to what he has to say first."

"Complicated!"

"Complicated is only a word, but Methie has faith in you, and that will help! As far as I'm concerned, you have sheep-like tendencies. You are easily brainwashed, and you find it easier to keep the fire burning than to put it out and start again, even though you know it's wrong!"

"We need to learn your ways, Fax. We need to learn how to grow machines!"

"I'm warning you, Bertie. Goat wouldn't tolerate less than full cooperation; he had ways to inspire us. A positive mental attitude is key, and if there is any question with one's positivity, you will be taken and shown the truth."

"The truth?" Bertie raised an inquisitive eyebrow.

"Basically, you are taken to the edge of space and shown the Earth against the infinite blackness. And if that doesn't flick your switch, then gravity will soon be an inspiration, as suddenly you appreciate the antigravity equations!" Fax laughed.

"He dropped you?"

"He, it, who, what, yes, like a stone. Quite fun, really!"

"The School of the Technically Gifted, that is what we should call the school where people can learn your technology," interrupted Bertie.

"You are human; there is no such thing as the technically gifted; you're either eaten or not!" Fax commented instantly, warming to the idea.

Bertie thought of another name. "The School of Science, Ingenuity and Expansion!"

"You are missing the point. Most will have their training off world, and once you have experienced that, it will be hard to return! It was The Troodon School of Goat when I was alive."

"What about food, Fax? What are people going to eat. You said about banning grazers?"

"It's not going to happen overnight, Bertie; relax. But you don't need to chop the forest down, do you?"

"I like a juicy steak," moaned Bertie. "Can you talk to the leaders out there?"

"Yes, sure. After all, I'm here to help," Fax said sarcastically. "I don't suppose fifty years is all that long!" he added with a resolve in his mind.

"I'll be dead by then," Bettie mumbled sadly.

"Yes, we can't all be infinites now, can we? The effect of one generation affects the next, and as you will not be here to see it, I will oversee its progression."

Fax gave Bertie a reassuring cuddle and addressed the leaders, who were full of thanks.

Fax paused and took in a large breath. "Education, education, education, my school on Earth is going to be called 'The Environmental School of Fax and the Graphene Phenomenon.' I have a way to shock even the laziest of your children into the willingness to learn. But first you do realise you can grow steaks the size of houses and you won't be able to tell the difference, right?"

"The size of houses?" repeated the American president, licking his lips.

"Yes, Bertie here was worried." Fax pointed at the British prime minister, who liked the name of the school.

"There is no time for questions, so I am simply saying this. Within the fifty years you, I, we need to return the land to how it once was. I can't see the problem; you have been chasing deer in and around the forests since the beginning of time. Also, I'm going to show you how to grow houses from the atmosphere; it's much easier in space, as the graphene layers itself, but nevertheless, you can even grow an elevator to the moon with this stuff; it's easy if you know how. To build and travel without exhaust pipes is the key!"

Fax then sensed that Methie was waiting at the portcullis, and she wanted letting in.

The leaders started chatting amongst themselves; it was generally a can-do conversation.

"Oh yes, exhaust pipes! Simple to many. What's the matter with your legs? See, Bertie? That's what the sheep comment refers to. I've seen people leave their heated homes, expel exhaust fumes in a car journey to go to the local store and buy a packet of fags, and they only live two hundred metres away!" he said sarcastically as he walked to the portcullis. "Whom amongst the lot of you drove here, hmm?"

"The use of a car is fundamental to life!" snapped the Russian president.

Fax held the Russian president's comment in his quantum as he raised the portcullis to invite the young man in. Fax looked into his eyes. "If only they would have listened to you. Then there wouldn't have been such a problem. Lay low for a while. I will call for you in a moment."

Fax returned and looked into the Russians president's eyes. "My drones move; they don't burn."

"How am I going to get back to Russia?"

"What? Now the rich have used up all the fuel just for one last holiday?" Fax snapped.

"I was hoping you were going to give me a lift!" Something assumed not only by the Russian president.

Fax smiled. "After all, I'm here to help!" he said sarcastically again.

"Is there any chance we can see Methie, Fax?" asked the Chinese president

"Methie? Methie has already made her choice; if she hasn't appeared, then she won't. There is only one human she likes other than Amazing, but he shares her realm and already is making the transaction into an infinite. It's his braincells see; they are beautiful."

Fax paused. "I present to you Sir David Frederick Attenborough. He is going to be the new headmaster of The Environmental School of Fax and the Graphene Phenomenon."

Sir David walked out from the jewel house. "Hello, hello! Blooming strange this getting younger lark; it comes highly recommended, by the way; kind of extraordinary after such a long life. I feel fantastic."

"He is going to live forever. This television presenter and you are going to leave us all to die," muttered all the politicians.

"Methie doesn't care for much else. He has been telling you for years about the fragile nature of the Earth, and you have put a price on her head. If I had my way, I would kill the lot of you or time travel back one hundred thousand years and stop you leaving Africa. There really is no point to you if you are only going to kill yourselves. Think about it, dah. You have fifty years. We need to educate a generation on how the drones are grown from graphene and understand how versatile it is.

"The replanting of the forests and flowers native to your regions is a start. The oceans need to restock, as the volcano will affect them. There will be no more drilling or mining; extract what is needed from Yellowstone. This might be a bit strict, but the human population needs to be restricted to only the brightest hair heads while you are still bound to the Earth. Mars will need seeding, and Venus will need taming.

"Basically, nature lovers you were and need to be again. It's your combined knowledge as a species that will enable you to utilise the expanse of space. Don't think for one minute this is all hocus-pocus and fairy dust baloney sausage. There is evidence in the galaxy of species eating their planet and rendering it unhabitable. The metal from the caldera will help you forge moulds for spaceships. Mars will need to be your second home. I want to see you fly across the heavens—why else do you think an intelligent species evolves out from the conscious ether? It's not to kill its mother, I can assure you of that. I will help you. I will help you understand our technology so that you can become true intelligence."

It was at that moment that Fax indicated it was the end of the conversation and made arrangements for the leaders to return to their respected countries by drone. Fax then returned to Kyle and the professor, who he found in a pub called The Gates of Hell on the Gibraltar coast.

"That will take years to cool," Fax said as he walked in as old chisel face, peering over their shoulders.

"It was her, the one you spoke of, Methiemauritania?" Kyle realised.

"See? Fax never lies."

"Yellowstone went off six hundred thousand years ago and six hundred before that. I could have told them it was going to explode, but no one would listen. No one knew except you. I love you, Fax. I love you!" cuddled a drunk professor.

"How much has he had to drink?"

"Not enough, nowhere near enough. We're celebrating. You would get mobbed if they knew it was you, you old beauty!"

"Yes, well, we have got things to do."

***

The next morning, Kyle and the professor awoke inside their sleeping bags on makeshift beds. Fax was soon to acknowledge their awareness.

"You are in a drone—a fighter drone, to be more accurate. Lovely, isn't it?"

Kyle noticed that they were racing across a snow-covered land below. There was little if any sound, and Kyle prompted the professor to take a look.

"By Jove, where in the blue blazes are we?" asked the professor.

"We are over Antarctica, heading towards the pole. I need to meet Goat before he decides to do something that could turn out unfortunate."

"I thought you said you would rather he didn't interfere?"

"I didn't call him," Fax mused.

Suddenly, the craft came to a controlled hover, and Fax disconnected himself from the drone.

"It's minus fifty degrees outside. I suggest you wait here." Fax dropped through the transparent force field and onto the ice surface below.

Kyle and the professor watched as he melted his way down. Fax dropped to bedrock and instantly formed a cavern with a gold blast to reveal a dormant-looking drone street. He activated one of the drones, retreated to the surface and continued their journey.

"Do you mind me asking who could have called him?"

Fax looked at Kyle with a long serious stare. "Methie could have, I suppose, but I thought she was happy. I have just sent him a text."

At the pole, a figure stood. Fax again jumped through the force field. The ice crunched under his feet, and he could see Goat smiling as he approached. Suddenly, the angelic appearance of Methie stood, and they started to hold a conversation. Methie was soon to disappear and left Goat looking like he was in pain. Fax raced forward to hold him, but as he did, he felt a power surge in his mind. The cave full of what were bats was no longer. It was like each bat had stored information and, as fast as lightning, pictures started to flash within his quantum. Fax zoomed to places he had never been, times he had never seen. Mathematical equations downloaded beyond the speed of light until it came to an end. Fax felt charged, even though he had been on a golden diet.

"You are all that was me now. You have made me proud, my boy, proud. I've had enough of that conscious forever rubbish! I can die now. Methie allowed this because of you."

Fax held Goat in his arms as he changed from Troodon to human.

"It's bloody freezing!" came from the young, half-naked human Fax was holding. "Get me on the drone before I freeze to death!" asked Goat.

Fax, slightly shocked but in awe of what was before him, entered the drone and looked at Kyle and the professor looking back at him.

"This is Kyle Hamish Thyme, and this is Professor Woodrow Malarkey," Fax said, delighted.

They looked at the person before them, and he spoke. "You can call me George, because that is my name!"

***

Six months later, the drones had been transformed into learning centres along the nature corridors, and the planet's children were attending. But there was rumour of a growing discontent coming from the older generation, and leaders alike were finding it too hard to adjust. The once rich and wealthy were demanding justice, as there was now need to get their pristine hands dirty. The leaders called on Fax many a time to let them talk to Methie, but he was failing to satisfy their demands.

"This is all a joke" was reverberating around the airwaves. "Fax is a hoax." "It was trick photography." "Methie isn't real" was also echoing its doubts. Parents started to question the authority of the schools, and there was a sense that rebellion was rising.

But Methie couldn't be reached. It was a conversation with his former master that gave him an idea.

Fax called for the leaders of the world to meet in London, where he would try to appease their demands. If Fax couldn't call on Methie to come to him, then Fax was going to go to her. The plan was hatched and the time set.

Worker drones picked up the leaders and hovered above the Tower of London. Fax took a fighter drone and flew into the middle, where they all converged into one. He asked if anyone wanted refreshments and for everyone to be seated while he took them out of the atmosphere and into space. The mother drone stopped at half the distance the moon was from the Earth.

Fax then asked for silence, as Earth appeared in a giant window. She hung beautiful within the infinite black. It was at that moment that a solar flare could be seen glittering towards her.

"Behold . . . I give you Methie!"

The leaders were wowed with what they saw. It was for no longer than a couple of seconds, but they saw the wings of an angel shrouding, protecting the Earth from the sun's cosmic radiation. The flare was powerful, forcing her to shine brighter than ever before.

Fax said, "Yet again she has saved you. You have fifty years, or you with be left to burn in a Venus-like hell. It's simple; we have to work together to lower the legacy of your emissions, or else the volcano will cause a runaway greenhouse effect and the death of your children! Is that what you want? Are you with me?"

To be Continued

Review Requested:

We'd like to know if you enjoyed the book.
Please consider leaving a review on the platform
from which you purchased the book.